90

J 812 Bra

Bradley, Virginia, 1912-

Holidays on stage :

$8.^{95}$

HOLIDAYS ON STAGE

A Festival of Special-Occasion Plays

Other Books by Virginia Bradley

Bend to the Willow

Is There an Actor in the House?
Dramatic Material from Pantomime to Play

Stage Eight
One-Act Plays

HOLIDAYS ON *STAGE*

A Festival of Special-Occasion Plays

Virginia Bradley

DODD, MEAD & COMPANY
NEW YORK

If these plays are not given for profit, they
may be used for live performances without permission.
For profit-making productions, permission must be
obtained from the publisher.

1   2   3   4   5   6   7   8   9   10

Library of Congress Cataloging in Publication Data

Bradley, Virginia, date
Holidays on stage.

    Contents: The night that time sat still—A ground-
hog by any other name—The big red heart—[etc.]
    1. Holidays—Juvenile drama.   2. Children's plays,
American.   [1. Holidays—Drama.   2. Plays]   I. Title.
PS3552.R233H6   812'.54   81-43225
ISBN 0-396-07993-8   AACR2

To Michael, my son
and my invaluable critic,
with love and appreciation

CONTENTS

THE NIGHT THAT
TIME SAT STILL

THE NIGHT THAT TIME SAT STILL

CHARACTERS

FATHER TIME

ERMAGRACE RALSTON, WHO IS TWELVE

THE OLD YEAR

HERKY, A TRAMP

BEAU, A TRAMP WITH CLASS

MRS. RALSTON, ERMAGRACE'S MOTHER

AUNT HARRIET

JUDGE RALSTON, ERMAGRACE'S FATHER

UNCLE HUGO

THE NEW YEAR

FATHER TIME *enters from the right in front of the closed curtain. He is the traditionally accepted figure with long white beard, flowing robe, and a scythe over his shoulder. He is obviously looking for someone or something, and he is also obviously cold in his flimsy attire. He constantly moves about as he peers first out to the audience and then offstage left.* ERMAGRACE RALSTON *runs toward the stage from the back of the theater. She is wearing a winter coat and a stocking cap, and around her neck she has a bright colored muffler. She is also carrying a book in one mittened hand.*

ERMAGRACE. (*Sees* FATHER TIME *when she reaches the foot of the stage steps and calls out to him*) Hey, there. What are you looking for?

FATHER TIME. (*who was looking off into the wings, turns, startled*) Oh, you startled me. I don't usually make appearances in public, and I didn't think anybody would be around who could see me. (*He continues to keep his body in motion, sometimes jogging in place, sometimes doing a marching step.*)

ERMAGRACE. (*coming on to the stage*) You're out here in plain sight, for goodness sake. Anybody could see you.

FATHER TIME. You're wrong there. Not just anybody. You must be one of The Extraordinaries.

ERMAGRACE. Extraordinaries? If that means what I think it does, you're wrong. You wouldn't say I was anything special if you looked in at my house. No one pays any attention to me. (*changes the subject*) Say, aren't you cold?

FATHER TIME. This is the coldest December 31st I've ever seen.

ERMAGRACE. You ought to have a coat. I wouldn't be allowed out of the house without one. Mine's brand new. (*She models it with a professional air.*) Doesn't it look elegant?

FATHER TIME. I think it looks warm. (*He shivers as he moves about.*)

ERMAGRACE. You definitely shouldn't be out on New Year's Eve in a—in a nightgown.

FATHER TIME. Of course I shouldn't—be out, that is—and I don't have much choice about what to wear. It isn't a nightgown though. Somebody got the idea I was supposed to look like this and I'm stuck with it.

ERMAGRACE. I don't understand. Why do you have to look like that? (*She indicates his clothes.*)

FATHER TIME. Because I'm Father Time, that's why. And the clothes are bad enough without having to carry this ridiculous thing around with me (*He holds up the scythe.*) since the beginning of time, and that, if my point is clear, is since the beginning of me.

ERMAGRACE. So you're Father Time. I should have recognized you.

FATHER TIME. (*looks more closely at her*) Yes, you should have. You're one of The Extraordinaries all right. I'm sure of it.

ERMAGRACE. I still don't understand why you say that. And you know there's something else I don't understand. Why do you have to be *Father* Time? If you were *Mother* Time I'll bet you wouldn't be out here without a coat. And why do you keep hopping around?

FATHER TIME. You know Time never stands still. It's against the rules. Look, if we're going to be critical, what are you doing out after dark?

ERMAGRACE. I had permission—sort of. I was across the street at my friend's house. We were going to wait for the New Year together, but she got sleepy and went to bed. There wasn't anything for me to do but go home. I didn't realize how late it was. (*changes the subject*) I really wasn't criticizing, you know. I don't suppose it's altogether your fault that women are neglected.

FATHER TIME. It certainly isn't. I have been working on some ideas along that line for years, but I can't change things all by myself. Maybe if there were more young people like you it would be easier.

ERMAGRACE. (*follows along behind him, mimicking whatever movement he makes*) There you go again—talking as though I was important. When your mother's the president of the P.T.A. and your father's a judge, always tied up in court or with his nose in his musty law books, you don't count for much. Particularly when you're only twelve—not even a teenager.

FATHER TIME. All that has nothing to do with it. Besides you do count with your parents. You just told me you weren't allowed out in the cold without a coat. What's your name?

ERMAGRACE. Ermagrace Ralston.

FATHER TIME. (*nods enthusiastically*) Of course. You're Judge Ralston's girl. That figures. Well, Ermagrace Ralston, you wouldn't be able to see me if you weren't special. What's more, you've got make-believe in your eyes. On most days I'll bet you aren't even Ermagrace

Ralston. You're somebody else—somebody you dream up. Right?

ERMAGRACE. How did you know that?

FATHER TIME. It's a first qualification.

ERMAGRACE. Yesterday I was Felicia, Queen of the Silver Skates. I was practicing for the Olympics. (*She pantomimes skating.*)

FATHER TIME. I'm sure you were in top form.

ERMAGRACE. Just fair. But last Saturday I was the general manager of Disneyland.

FATHER TIME. Oh, that's a good one.

ERMAGRACE. On Sundays I'm usually a writer. My mother says I have a wild imagination.

FATHER TIME. First qualification, all right.

ERMAGRACE. My father says imagination is important for a writer. He even gave me this book for Christmas. (*holds the book up for him to see*) All blank pages. I can write my own stories in it. I took it over to show my friend. She'd never seen a book like that.

FATHER TIME. Excellent.

ERMAGRACE. (*thoughtfully*) Some days, though, I spend a
lot of time just thinking.

FATHER TIME. That, Ermagrace Ralston, is the second qualification.

ERMAGRACE. My mother calls it lollygagging, but my father
laughs and says that's another word for dreaming. He
doesn't seem to think that's too bad.

FATHER TIME. Ah, it's the young dreamers who shape the
future of the world. The sad thing is we often lose those
dreamers when they grow up.

ERMAGRACE. Sometimes I don't think I'll ever get past
twelve.

FATHER TIME. I wouldn't worry about that if I were you.

(FATHER TIME *shifts the scythe to his other shoulder.*)

ERMAGRACE. I suppose I oughtn't. I'll be thirteen next year.
It's just that time goes by like a crippled snail.

FATHER TIME. (*offended*) You're being critical again.

ERMAGRACE. I'm sorry. I didn't mean to hurt your feelings.
But could you hurry things up a little?

FATHER TIME. That's what I'm out to do right now. I really
shouldn't have stopped to talk. There's something

wrong. I seem to be slowing down. It's very upsetting, and *he's* probably responsible.

ERMAGRACE. Who?

FATHER TIME. The Old Year, of course. I can't explain now. I have to find him before it's too late. (*He shivers again.*) I wish it weren't so cold.

ERMAGRACE. If you're going to stay out in this weather, you'll have to have something to put around you. Look, you can borrow my muffler.

FATHER TIME. Don't you need it?

ERMAGRACE. I'm practically home. Right there. (*She motions toward the right exit. Then she takes off the muffler and winds it around* FATHER TIME's *neck.*) Isn't that better?

FATHER TIME. Much better. And I'll get it back to you. As soon as I locate that rascal and straighten out a few things. (*He pulls the muffler closer around his neck and heads for the left exit.*)

ERMAGRACE. (*calling after him*) Better hurry if you expect to catch the Old Year. You certainly don't have much time. (*After he is offstage, she looks out to the audience.*) That was a silly thing for me to say. He's all the time there is. (*She runs offstage right.*)

The curtain opens on the den in the Ralston house. There is a fireplace upstage center with a draped window on each side of it. At center stage, two large armchairs face each other with a coffee table between them. There is a straight chair and perhaps a desk at stage right and other furnishings as desired.

As soon as the curtain opens, the window upstage left is pushed up and the OLD YEAR *enters, climbing over the sill. He is wearing jeans, a heavy jacket and a cap, which is pulled low over his eyes. He takes off the jacket to reveal a T-shirt with the current year printed across both the back and the front of it. Draping the jacket over his shoulders, he moves about the room, glancing furtively behind him as though afraid of being followed. There are sounds from outside the window where he himself entered, and he turns to see* HERKY *and* BEAU *climb over the sill and come into the room.* HERKY *wears old baggy clothes. He is unshaven and unkempt. In fact, he looks like the tramp that he is.* BEAU, *on the other hand, although also a vagrant with clothes that are shabby and unpressed, wears a morning coat, striped trousers and a battered top hat. All with the air of a man of importance.*

OLD YEAR. Pardon me. I know why I came in that way. Somebody's after me. I had to find a place I could hide. But ordinary people don't usually come in through the window, do they? (HERKY *and* BEAU *obviously neither see nor hear him and there is no answer.*)

HERKY. (*looking around*) This ain't no bedroom, Beau.

BEAU. (*whose speech matches his attempted elegance of dress*) That, my friend, is a fine point of observation. It is not a boudoir. By some unfortunate miscalculation, we have selected the wrong ingress.

HERKY. I think we got the wrong window.

(*They continue to walk around the room looking things over.*)

OLD YEAR. (*persists*) The only reason an ordinary person would come through a window would be because he forgot his key. I'll bet you never had a key. Did you?

(*They still, of course, pay no attention to him.*)

HERKY. What we gonna do now, Beau?

OLD YEAR. I suggest you leave the way you came. You won't answer my questions. I don't think you belong here.

HERKY. Are you thinkin' what to do, Beau?

BEAU. Silence, my friend. It occurs to me that we might be able to locate the boudoir.

HERKY. You said it was gonna be easy, Beau. You said these people got a party goin'. We sneak in the bedroom window, take all the pocketbooks, and sneak out again. Easy as pie, you said.

BEAU. I said refrain from speech, my friend, while I cogitate.

OLD YEAR. So that's it. You plan to steal. As if I haven't had enough of that kind of thing.

HERKY. (*hearing a sound offstage left*) Whatever you're gonna do, Beau, you better do it fast. Somebody's comin'.

OLD YEAR. You aren't paying a bit of attention to me.

BEAU. It is my considered opinion that we should conceal ourselves to avoid a visual confrontation.

HERKY. I'm gonna hide.

> (*They hide behind the drapes at the left window. The* OLD YEAR *gets behind the armchair at right center as* MRS. RALSTON *enters from the left, walking quickly and with irritation. She is followed by* ERMAGRACE *who has taken off her mittens but still wears the coat and cap and has her book in hand.*)

MRS. RALSTON. My it's cold in here. (*She goes to left window which has not been closed.*) And no wonder. (*She closes the window and moves over to check the right one as she talks. She apparently cannot see the* OLD YEAR *who would be in her view.*) You know, Ermagrace, you shouldn't have walked home alone at this hour. You should have called us.

ERMAGRACE. I'm sorry. But I was just across the street.

> (*The* OLD YEAR, *who has decided no one can see him, pokes his head over the top of the chair to listen.* ERMAGRACE *does see him but says nothing.*)

MRS. RALSTON. That makes no difference. (*Her mind is already on something else. She goes to the clock on the mantel.*) I wonder what's the matter with the clocks in this house. I know they are all running slow. Our guests have certainly been here longer than an hour. Your Aunt Harriet has already eaten a whole plate of sandwiches, and Uncle Hugo is almost as bad at the punch bowl. Your father's refilled it three times. (*back to* ERMAGRACE) And where is your muffler, Ermagrace? I suppose you left it at your friend's.

ERMAGRACE. No—I—I lent it to somebody, but he said he'd get it back to me.

MRS. RALSTON. He? He who? (*horrified*) Oh, Ermagrace, you might have been kidnapped. Your father said there were a couple of vagrants up in his court just last week.

ERMAGRACE. I wasn't in any danger, Mother. I knew him. (*aside*) At least I should have known him.

MRS. RALSTON. (*relieved*) Well, that's something. Who was it, dear?

ERMAGRACE. Father Time. He's out looking for the Old Year.

MRS. RALSTON. Ermagrace! I don't know why you invent such stories. All right, so the muffler's lost. You'll not get a new one I'm afraid. Father Time! (*She shakes her head, then changes the subject.*) Now you can stay up until midnight if you wish. We'll be in the living room and you'll have the whole den to yourself. There's plenty of food in the kitchen, *if* I can hold back your Aunt Harriet. And remember you are to go to bed by twelve-thirty.

ERMAGRACE. Yes, Mother. (MRS. RALSTON *exits left and after she is gone* ERMAGRACE *moves to center stage and confronts the* OLD YEAR.) OK. You might as well come out.

> (*When she says this* BEAU *and* HERKY, *thinking she is talking to them, poke their heads out from opposite sides of the drapes.* ERMAGRACE *is not in a position to see them, and although the* OLD YEAR *does, he has other things on his mind. When* HERKY *and* BEAU *realize that* ERMAGRACE *is apparently talking to someone at the other side of the room they shrug and pull back into their hiding places.*)

OLD YEAR. (*coming out from behind the chair*) Do you mean me?

ERMAGRACE. Certainly. You're the one who's hiding.

OLD YEAR. Well, that's a relief. At least someone knows I exist. No one else seems to—they look right through me.

ERMAGRACE. Not that again. I can see you. And it's been explained to me—I think. By the way, Father Time's hunting all over for you. He's terribly upset. What's going on? What's wrong?

OLD YEAR. Everything's wrong, and he isn't any more upset than I am. I've had nothing but trouble. Right now there are two . . . (*He is interrupted by a shout from* FATHER TIME, *who has opened the window at the right of the fireplace and now leans into the room.*)

FATHER TIME. There you are! (*He climbs awkwardly over the sill, trying to cope with the scythe at the same time.*) You might at least give me a hand.

(*The* OLD YEAR *ignores the plea, crosses to the other chair at left center and stands behind it.* FATHER TIME *tumbles into the room, dropping the scythe as he does so.* ERMAGRACE *runs to his assistance, helps him to his feet, and brushes him off.*)

ERMAGRACE. I hope you didn't hurt yourself.

FATHER TIME. (*pushing her gently aside*) I'm all right. (*He picks up the scythe and moves toward the* OLD YEAR.) Don't you know you were supposed to check in this morning?

OLD YEAR. (*from the protection of the chair*) Just you let me alone.

FATHER TIME. I've never had trouble like this before. You should be getting ready for the New Year. There are "watch" parties going on all over the country.

ERMAGRACE. There's one right here. (*She gestures off to the left.*)

FATHER TIME. (*ignores the remark and speaks to the* OLD YEAR) You're expected to make a dramatic exit. You know that. (*He turns and paces off to the right.*)

OLD YEAR. (*quietly*) I've decided not to leave.

FATHER TIME. (*He hasn't caught the announcement and goes right on talking.*) You're not dressed right and you haven't even packed. (*Suddenly he realizes what the* OLD YEAR *has said and he turns on him.*) What did you say?

OLD YEAR. I said, I'm not going.

FATHER TIME. That's ridiculous. Of course you're going. It's the way of things.

OLD YEAR. It isn't going to be my way. I haven't been the least bit satisfied with my term here. From January to December I've shouldered all kinds of disaster, faced rebellion, crime, and a million disappointments. Where were the good things?

ERMAGRACE. We just had the brightest holidays in the year.

FATHER TIME. And have you forgotten Thanksgiving and the Fourth of July? And spring?

OLD YEAR. All routine. You could have handled them without me. There should have been special things. 1969 had the walk on the moon. 1863, bad as he had it with full-scale Civil War, could at least boast the end of slavery. Even old 1620 had the safe landing of the *Mayflower.*

FATHER TIME. Those things have all been done. Besides, every year can't be spectacular.

OLD YEAR. (*pouting*) I didn't expect world peace or anything like that, but you could have arranged something for me. I simply will not be pushed out and flattened into the history books without a single memorable credit. I've decided to stay on, come what may.

ERMAGRACE. I don't see how you can do that.

FATHER TIME. He can't. (*to the* OLD YEAR) There's no use arguing about it. You have to go. It is my duty to see that you do. (*He moves toward the* OLD YEAR *brandishing the scythe.*)

OLD YEAR. I won't let you put me out. (*He dodges* FATHER TIME *who continues to stalk him.*)

ERMAGRACE. You two go ahead and fight about it. I'm hungry. I'm going to get some food. (*She exits right to the kitchen and* BEAU *pokes his head out from behind the drapes and looks around. Since he cannot see* FATHER TIME *and the* OLD YEAR, *he emerges.*)

FATHER TIME. (*sees* BEAU *and stops in his pursuit of the* OLD YEAR) Who's he?

OLD YEAR. More trouble. There are two of them. They're robbers. I tried to get them to leave, but they paid no attention to me.

BEAU. (*to* HERKY) You may emerge now. The child has departed. (HERKY *comes out looking skeptical and* FATHER TIME, *who has been walking around* BEAU, *sizing him up, now looks* HERKY *over as well.*)

FATHER TIME. Of course they paid no attention. They can't see *or* hear us. They are not Extraordinaries. If you'd read your manual you would have known that.

(HERKY *is looking all around, under the chairs and tables.*)

OLD YEAR. Maybe you should tell the girl.

FATHER TIME. First things first. They look harmless enough. I'll take care of them as soon as we have you ready to go. (*Once again, he moves toward the* OLD YEAR.)

HERKY. She was talkin' to somebody.

BEAU. Observe. There is no one in the room.

HERKY. Then was she talkin' to herself, Beau? Huh? Was she, huh? I knew a guy what talked to hisself once. A looney.

BEAU. Not to worry, friend. Perhaps if we venture in this direction. (*He heads toward the left exit as Aunt Harriet's voice is heard offstage.*)

AUNT HARRIET. (*offstage left*) We need more sandwiches, folks. I'll get some. Be right back.

BEAU. On second thought, we'd better retreat once again to our place of concealment. (*They get behind the drapes again as* AUNT HARRIET *enters from the left and* ERMAGRACE *comes back into the room from the right with a tray of sandwiches, punch, and glasses. All the while* FATHER TIME *is trying to catch the* OLD YEAR *who still manages to elude him.*)

AUNT HARRIET. (*descends on* ERMAGRACE *and takes the plate of sandwiches from the tray*) You were just bringing those to me now, weren't you, sweetie? You must have known we were out. (*She kisses* ERMAGRACE *on the cheek and starts toward the left exit.*)

FATHER TIME. (*to the* OLD YEAR) If you'd just listen to reason, old fellow.

OLD YEAR. Reason. That's what I do listen to—my reason for not leaving.

AUNT HARRIET. (*turns at the exit*) Did you say something, sweetie?

ERMAGRACE. (*realizing it was* FATHER TIME *and the* OLD YEAR *she might have heard*) No. I didn't say anything.

AUNT HARRIET. Hmmm. Hugo says I imagine things. Maybe I do. I was sure . . . (*changes the subject*) Why don't you come into the other room? Join the party.

ERMAGRACE. No thanks, Aunt Harriet. I'm all right here. (AUNT HARRIET *exits and* ERMAGRACE *turns to* FATHER TIME *with surprise.*) Could she hear you?

FATHER TIME. Only with her heart. Dear old Harriet. She had a lot of promise once, but she got sidetracked while she was still a young girl. She met Hugo and he put a damper on her dreams. The Extraordinaries often get sidetracked one way or another.

ERMAGRACE. Well, you can see how special I am. Aunt Harriet took my sandwiches. At least she left the punch. It's getting late. (*to the* OLD YEAR) You know the only way you can possibly stick around is by stopping time.

OLD YEAR. I'm prepared to do that if I have to. (*He produces an old blunderbuss from inside his jacket.*)

ERMAGRACE. You wouldn't!

OLD YEAR. If it's the only way.

FATHER TIME. (*to* OLD YEAR) I believe you're serious. You just haven't thought about the consequences.

OLD YEAR. I've thought about one thing. I'm simply not going. I'll stay and find out what's ahead.

FATHER TIME. If you destroy me, there's nothing ahead. You'll be right in this room forever.

OLD YEAR. You're trying to frighten me. Why can't I leave this room—this house?

FATHER TIME. It would take time and there will be no more time. Remember?

OLD YEAR. Well, at least no one will be able to look back and say I was a bad year. No one will be in a position to look back.

FATHER TIME. That's right. Everyone will just stay here and say you *are* a bad year—and keep wishing you were gone. Besides, think of the new one out there in the cold with no hope of coming in.

OLD YEAR. I'm sorry about that, but . . .

ERMAGRACE. You mean the new year won't ever come in? I'll never get to be thirteen?

OLD YEAR. I'm sorry about that too, but I'm afraid it's the only way. I have to think of myself. At least I'll be here.

FATHER TIME. Oh, you'll be here, all right. You and Ermagrace and those two behind the curtain. You're willing to share "forever" with those unsavory characters?

ERMAGRACE. What unsavory characters? What are you talking about?

FATHER TIME. (*to* OLD YEAR) Tell her.

OLD YEAR. You just want to get my mind off my purpose. (*He is having trouble keeping the gun on* FATHER TIME *who constantly moves about.*)

ERMAGRACE. Well, somebody tell me.

OLD YEAR. I guess you might as well know. There are a couple of tramps behind the drapes. They said they were here to steal from your guests.

ERMAGRACE. We'll see about that. (*Completely unafraid, she moves toward the drapes.*) OK, you two. Come out of there with your hands up. (*She glances toward the* OLD YEAR.) We have a gun.

(HERKY *and* BEAU *come out sheepishly with their hands up.*)

HERKY. We wasn't goin' to do anything. Honest. Was we, Beau?

BEAU. Only wish you a Happy New Year, dear girl. As you see, we are unarmed. (*He sees that she has no gun.*) And I observe, dear girl, that you hold no firearm either. (*He starts to bring his hands down.*)

ERMAGRACE. Put your hands right back in the air. Shall we prove that you are covered? (*She looks at the* OLD YEAR.) We have a gun all right, and we also have another kind of weapon—a sharp one. (*She glances at* FATHER TIME'S *scythe.* BEAU *hesitates a moment and then puts his hands back in the air.*)

HERKY. What does she mean "we"?

ERMAGRACE. You should be ashamed of yourselves. Just as soon as we get this other business taken care of I'll call my father. He'll know what to do with you.

FATHER TIME. It probably won't make any difference if he uses that thing. (*He indicates the* OLD YEAR *and the blunderbuss.*)

ERMAGRACE. I wish you wouldn't say that.

HERKY. I wish we was out of here. She's talkin' to somebody again, and there ain't nobody.

BEAU. Hmmm. It is an unnerving situation.

ERMAGRACE. You aren't going to let him get away with it?

FATHER TIME. Actually, Ermagrace Ralston, it's all up to you.

ERMAGRACE. What can I do?

FATHER TIME. In a crisis, it's always up to The Extraordinaries. But you'll have to hurry.

ERMAGRACE. I've never had to dream myself out of a thing like this. I need to think. (*She crosses to right stage and stands with her back to the others.*)

BEAU. (*whispers to* HERKY) I think we might just leave. She's only a girl.

ERMAGRACE. I heard that. (*to* OLD YEAR) Shoot if they make a move.

HERKY. You can go if you want. I'm scared.

ERMAGRACE. And watch the smooth one. I don't like his looks.

BEAU. I, too, shall remain as I am. (*He keeps his hands up.*)

ERMAGRACE. (*still speaking to the* OLD YEAR) I've got an idea. Suppose I could make you remembered forever. Would you leave?

OLD YEAR. I don't see how you can manage that. It's too late. (*He moves closer to* FATHER TIME *and takes aim.*)

ERMAGRACE. Don't do it! Think of your choices. Stay as you are now, frozen here like this and despised forever. Or take my offer.

OLD YEAR. Are you sure I'll have a memorable credit in the history books?

ERMAGRACE. Better than that. I promise.

OLD YEAR. All right. But the town clock is beginning to strike. (*There is the sound of the clock offstage.*) What can you do?

ERMAGRACE. You'll see. But first I'll take this thing. (*She takes the gun and puts it on the coffee table. Then she takes her muffler from around Father Time's neck as she speaks to him.*) I've got to do it—stop you—but it's better this way. It won't be permanent.

FATHER TIME. I have nothing to lose.

HERKY. You sure got us in the looney bin this time.

BEAU. Baffling. Utterly baffling.

> (*During* BEAU *and* HERKY'S *speeches,* ERMAGRACE *leads* FATHER TIME *to the straight chair at right stage and ties him to it with the muffler. The town*

clock has been striking, and it is between the eleventh and the twelfth strike that it stops. FATHER TIME *stops moving and* BEAU *and* HERKY *also become immobile. Only* ERMAGRACE *and the* OLD YEAR *can now speak and move.*)

ERMAGRACE. (*to the* OLD YEAR) Come on, sit down and have some punch. I have stopped Time. (*She fills two glasses, hands one to the* OLD YEAR, *and raises her own as in a toast before she puts it back on the table.*) Now you are immortalized.

OLD YEAR. Why now? I was going to stop him.

ERMAGRACE. Yes, with a gun. Everyone knows it isn't right to kill Time. This way you have simply held him back— the only year ever to have stayed the passage of Time.

OLD YEAR. Even so, I am not satisfied. You know that this is happening and I know it, but how will the world know it? When that town clock strikes once more it will all be fantasy.

ERMAGRACE. That's the most important part. They will know it, because I am going to be a writer and I will set down the story just as it happened—your story.

OLD YEAR. But what will I have to show the other years— what proof?

ERMAGRACE. I will give you my autograph—on the book, of course. (*She picks up the book her father had given her.*

*With a flourish she writes her name inside and hands it
to the* OLD YEAR.)

OLD YEAR. (*opens the book*) But the pages here are blank.

ERMAGRACE. Of course. And all the better. You are probably the only one ever to have an autographed copy of
a book that hasn't yet been written.

OLD YEAR. You will write it though? You promise me that?

ERMAGRACE. Of course I do. (*The* OLD YEAR *begins to
smile. He finishes off his punch and stands up as* ERMA-
GRACE *continues.*) And now there will be plenty of time.

OLD YEAR. (*who has moved to the window at left*) Well,
here I go.

ERMAGRACE. I just remembered you never did pack.

OLD YEAR. No matter. I have the only thing that's important. (*He holds up the book.*) I'm really glad it
worked out this way.

ERMAGRACE. So am I. I would have hated being twelve
forever. (ERMAGRACE *loosens the ties that hold* FATHER
TIME *and as he moves again the* OLD YEAR *exits through
the window and the town clock strikes the twelfth time.*)

FATHER TIME. Good girl. I couldn't have managed that.

(MRS. RALSTON *enters from the left.*)

MRS. RALSTON. Just wanted to wish you a Happy . . .
   (*She stops when she sees* HERKY *and* BEAU.) What . . .
   (JUDGE RALSTON *enters behind her and* HERKY *and* BEAU,
   *who are now released from immobility, react to his pres-
   ence.*)

HERKY. Ain't that the Judge, Beau?

BEAU. It would seem we selected more than the wrong window. We got the wrong house.

MRS. RALSTON. (*to the* JUDGE) Who are these men, dear?
   It wasn't to be a costume party.

JUDGE RALSTON. (*who has crossed to* HERKY *and* BEAU)
   What are you two doing here? I thought you were to be
   out of town by last Friday.

HERKY. We was just goin'.

BEAU. Precisely.

ERMAGRACE. They were going to steal, but we held a gun
   on them.

MRS. RALSTON. A gun? Nonsense. There are no guns in this
   house. Your father doesn't approve of keeping guns.

JUDGE RALSTON. (*who has been talking to the men*) I think
   you can put your hands down now.

HERKY. They won't shoot?

> (HUGO *and* AUNT HARRIET *enter from the left in time to hear* HERKY's *question.*)

HUGO. Shoot? What's he talking about?

JUDGE RALSTON. A little misunderstanding, Hugo. Why don't you take these fellows out to the kitchen and give them some food. Then we'll find a spot for them in the rooms over the garage until morning. After all it's a new year.

> (HUGO, *leading the way, heads for the right exit with* HERKY *and* BEAU.)

AUNT HARRIET. Happy New Year, Ermagrace. And you know, sweetie, the strangest thing happened. The town clock struck eleven times and then stopped for ever so long. It was weird. Time just seemed to stand still.

ERMAGRACE. *Sat* still, really.

HUGO. (*turns at the exit and speaks to* HARRIET) It was all in your head, Harriet. You just imagine things. (*exits with* HERKY *and* BEAU *following*)

AUNT HARRIET. Hugo never believes me.

MRS. RALSTON. Well, the new year is here, Ermagrace. Off to bed now. (*She sees and picks up the muffler.*) Oh, you found your muffler after all. Well, that's good. I do hate to be scolding you all the time. And you see it wasn't necessary to make up that silly story about Father Time.

ERMAGRACE. Yes, Mother. Happy New Year.

JUDGE RALSTON. We really came in just to wish you a Happy New Year. Better get back to the others. (MRS. RALSTON *and* AUNT HARRIET *exit left but the* JUDGE *lingers a minute. He picks up the gun which is still on the table.*) Hmm. I haven't seen one of these for a long time. Hmmm. Well, see you in the morning, Ermagrace. Happy New Year.

ERMAGRACE. Good night. Happy New Year. (*The* JUDGE *exits left and she turns to* FATHER TIME.) My father saw the gun—picked it up. Could he see you?

FATHER TIME. I think he might have. Your father has always been one of The Extraordinaries. That's why he is a good judge. He still has his dreams, but he's clever enough to live with the Hugos of the world. I trust the New Year will be good to him.

ERMAGRACE. The New Year! I forgot. Did he come in?

FATHER TIME. Indeed. Just waiting for you to ask.

(*The* NEW YEAR *enters from the right. It is a girl.*)

ERMAGRACE. It's a girl. The New Year is a *Girl*. (*to* FATHER TIME) You arranged that, didn't you?

FATHER TIME. It was the least I could do.

(*quick curtain*)

PRODUCTION NOTES

The Night That Time Sat Still is a fantasy and should be taken on with a light heart.

The opening scene in front of the closed curtain will depend for its success on the vitality of the two characters involved. The constant movement of Father Time should be varied and offers an opportunity for an imaginative director. Ermagrace, of course, has some independent action —modeling her coat and pantomiming the ice-skating. This, along with her mimicry of Father Time, will keep the scene alive. The dialogue will not have to carry the burden.

In the main body of the play, there is the added factor that some characters cannot be seen or heard by others. Again the director is important. The staging is tricky, but the result can be comical—Father Time's stalking the Old Year, for example, while Herky and Beau speak to each other unaware of the activity going on around them.

The costumes are quite well defined in the script. If the morning clothes indicated for Beau are not available, others might be substituted as long as it is suggested that he is a dandy. The Old Year's T-shirt shouldn't be a problem. A little black paint on an old white T-shirt should take care of it. Mrs. Ralston, Aunt Harriet, Judge Ralston, and Hugo are in contemporary dress suitable for a New Year's party. Remember the New Year is a little girl. It might be nice to give her ruffles and ribbons. Femininity is in again.

A check of the script will also provide a list of the necessary props. Of course, you won't want Father Time pursuing the Old Year with a real scythe. Perhaps one could be fashioned from sturdy cardboard. The gun is designated as a blunderbuss, and the purpose of the antiquated weapon is simply to uphold the fantasy element. The Old Year takes it from the inside of his jacket, and it would have to be secured there by loops or straps since it would be too big to fit in a pocket. If it is difficult to devise a blunderbuss, any preposterous-looking weapon you can come up with will work.

The play calls for a realistic set, but it is always possible to adapt to more limited facilities. A fireplace with a mantel is not absolutely vital. The clock can be on a bookcase. Windows seem necessary, at least some kind of frame through which the actors could climb, but again pantomime might suffice if an announcer explains the situation.

Lines, incidentally, can always be changed or adapted to fit your community. Mrs. Ralston could be president of some organization other than the P.T.A.

Be sure the striking of the town clock dovetails with the speeches and the action of the characters. It might take a bit of practice.

A GROUNDHOG BY
ANY OTHER NAME...

A GROUNDHOG BY ANY OTHER NAME . . .

CHARACTERS

RINEHART THE RABBIT
CARLEY COTTONTAIL
GROVER THE GROUNDHOG
WEJACK, THE LEADER OF THE GROUNDHOGS
OTCHUCK, FROM THE UNDERGROUND PRESS
OTHER GROUNDHOGS IN THE COMMUNITY

As the play begins, RINEHART *enters from the right in front of the closed curtain.*

RINEHART. (*Making his way across the stage toward the left exit, he sings an impromptu song to a tune of his own.*)
It's Groundhog Day in Punxsutawney,
It's Groundhog Day in all the land.

CARLEY. (*shouting from offstage right*) Groundhog Day! Hey, Rinehart, wait up. (*He enters from the right.*) What in the world are you singing about?

RINEHART. Groundhog Day, Carley. Don't you know it's the second of February?

CARLEY. What's that to you? You're no groundhog.

RINEHART. You think I don't know that? With these long ears. But today's the day the groundhog checks the weather. He comes out of his burrow after a long sleep and looks around. They say if he sees his shadow—whoosh—he's back in bed before you can twitch your whiskers, and we'll have six more weeks of winter. What's more . . .

CARLEY. (*interrupting with a sneer*) I've heard that story, but I still say what does it have to do with you?

RINEHART. Well, I got myself kind of involved with Grover the Groundhog.

CARLEY. Involved! Sometimes, Rinehart, I think you got nothing between those long ears of yours.

RINEHART. Just listen to me, Carley. You know that big black dog that runs wild around the meadow? Well, last October, about the time of the first fall of snow, that dog was after me. Believe me, I was running like a—like a rabbit.

CARLEY. You are a rabbit. You should stick to rabbits, Rinehart. Stay with your own kind I say. And what do you want to hang around with a groundhog for? He's a worthless creature.

RINEHART. It's a good thing the founding fathers of Punxsutawney can't hear you say that. And stop interrupting me. When I was running from that black dog, I was also running out of breath. Then I happened on this convenient little burrow . . . Come on, I'll tell you about it . . . (*They exit left as the curtain opens on the bur-row of* GROVER THE GROUNDHOG. *A large calendar, bear-ing the words "last October," hangs on the wall at center back. There is a low cot at center stage and a makeshift table beside it.* GROVER, *wearing a cap and trench coat, is sitting on the cot munching on an ear of corn. There is the sound of a dog barking offstage left and* RINEHART *makes a fast entrance from the left, star-tling the groundhog who drops his corn.*)

RINEHART. Whew! That was a close one.

GROVER. (*getting to his feet slowly and with great diffi-culty*) You're making rather free with my front door, aren't you? If I hadn't put on so much weight and if I weren't so very sleepy (*he yawns*), I'd nip that pink nose of yours.

RINEHART. Look here, I meant no harm and I'll be eternally grateful. That dog up there is enormous. I was never going to make it home. If I hadn't found your front door, it would have been the end of Rinehart the Rabbit. You have saved my life, Mr. Woodchuck.

GROVER. (*insulted*) Groundhog, if you don't mind.

RINEHART. Woodchuck—groundhog—all the same. What-ever you choose to call yourself, I pledge my indebted-ness. I will be forever your friend.

GROVER. I am a groundhog. I don't need a rabbit for a friend.

RINEHART. What a narrow point of view. But I will be your true friend whether you like it or not. That dog was almost as fast as I was. I am sorry, though, to break in on you. (*Now that* GROVER *is on his feet, he takes off his cap and coat and hangs them on a hook to the right of the calendar.*)

GROVER. (*yawns*) I suppose you're forgiven. I'm not partial to enormous dogs myself. But remember—it's *groundhog*. I definitely do not chuck wood and although I'm not a hog either, I prefer the sound of Grover the Groundhog. It grinds out nicely between my sharp teeth.

RINEHART. Whatever you say, but I am surprised to find you at home instead of at the gathering up there under the oak tree.

GROVER. Gathering? I wasn't notified of a gathering.

RINEHART. Hmmm. You must be new around here. You do know about Groundhog Day?

GROVER. Of course I do. But I *am* a newcomer, and where I hail from Groundhog Day isn't until February. Besides, what has Groundhog Day to do with the gathering?

RINEHART. Look, Grover my friend, I don't know where you hail from, but you're in Punxsutawney, and in Punxsutawney preparations for Groundhog Day are made with the fall of the first snow. Today is the day they name The Patsy.

GROVER. The what?

(*There is the sound of chatter offstage right.*)

RINEHART. Oh, oh, I am beginning to see a light. Forget that I said anything, Grover. Here they come.

(RINEHART *moves far downstage left where he will be unobserved by the groundhogs who enter from the right. Led by* WEJACK *and* OTCHUCK, *they wear caps and coats and carry picnic baskets. They are also fat and slow moving and yawn repeatedly.*)

WEJACK. We came in your back door, Grover. There was a big dog digging around at the front. Was he after you?

GROVER. No, thank goodness. Besides I think he's too big to get in.

WEJACK. Thank goodness for that too. We wouldn't want anything to happen to Grover, would we?

OTCHUCK. I should say not.

THE OTHER GROUNDHOGS. Hurray for Grover!

WEJACK. You see we have great news for you. You have just won the election.

GROVER. But I wasn't running for anything.

WEJACK. You were a scratch-in, Grover, and the vote was unanimous. We have come to celebrate. Bring out the food. We'll have one last feast before we hibernate.

(*They spread out food—corn, apples, greens—and they all begin to eat.*)

THE OTHER GROUNDHOGS. Here's to the Groundhog of the Year!

RINEHART. (*still unnoticed because the excitement of the moment is more important, now mutters to himself*) Poor fellow.

GROVER. Groundhog of the Year? What an honor for one who is new to your community.

WEJACK. That's reason to do you honor, Grover.

RINEHART. (*to himself again*) The very reason. Doesn't he know that?

OTCHUCK. As representative of the Underground Press, I am authorized to present the trophy. (*He produces a large shining trophy cup from one of the baskets and gives it to* GROVER *who accepts it with a bow which almost unbalances him.*)

THE OTHER GROUNDHOGS. Three cheers for Grover! King of the Weather Prophets.

GROVER. I am overwhelmed, but I still don't understand.

RINEHART. (*to himself*) He will. Oh, he will.

WEJACK. Now for the swearing in and the signing of the pact. (*He takes a scroll from one of the baskets and unrolls it.*) Do you, Grover, promise to fulfill the duties of Groundhog of the Year for the glory of our community and as a service to mankind?

GROVER. I do indeed. (*He is more interested in the trophy than in what he is saying.*) It is such a beautiful trophy.

WEJACK. Sign right here and the pledge is binding. (GROVER *signs and then tucks the scroll into the trophy cup.*) Everything is now in your hands. (*Several of the other groundhogs have already fallen asleep and the rest are yawning and trying to keep their eyes open.*) We can all sleep until spring. Let's go. (*Those who are awake help the others, and they all exit right.* GROVER, *who is also having a hard time staying awake, nonetheless dances around in a clumsy way and bumps into* RINEHART.)

GROVER. You still here? Well, you see who my friends are. Groundhog of the Year! Isn't that a fine thing?

RINEHART. Oh, it's a fine thing all right, Mr. King of the Weather Prophets—for all the others. Do you realize you didn't ask what your duties were, and you certainly didn't read what you signed. (*He takes the scroll from the trophy and hands it to* GROVER.)

GROVER. You read it. I seem to be having trouble keeping my eyes open.

RINEHART. (*reads*) "On February second, I"—that's you, Grover—"will come out of my snug little burrow and go up into the light of the early morning . . ."

GROVER. What's that?

RINEHART. You heard me. Up into the *cold* light of the *very* early morning.

GROVER. (*The truth finally dawns on him.*) Oh, no! You mean I've been elected to be *that* groundhog?

RINEHART. The very one. The Patsy. They had to trick somebody into taking the job.

GROVER. Well, I just won't accept it. (*He tucks his trophy under his arm and heads for the cot.*)

RINEHART. You already have. It's signed and sealed, and let me read the last paragraph. "And should I fail in my duties, I will be disgraced and exiled and doomed forever."

GROVER. Oh dear, I'm much too sleepy to think now. (*He crawls into his bed.*) Anyhow I'll never wake up, and they've made no provision for that.

RINEHART. You forget you saved my life, Grover. I am your friend.

GROVER. I don't want a rabbit for a friend. I just want to sleep.

RINEHART. All the same, you've got one. I will save you from disgrace. I will save you from exile. I will save you from doom. I will also save your trophy for you. On February second I will come to wake you. (GROVER *hasn't heard any of this speech. He is sound asleep and snoring. But* RINEHART *continues to talk.*) But how any creature can be smart enough to have a front door and a back door and still be so dumb is beyond me.

(*The curtain closes.*)

(RINEHART *and* CARLEY *come out in front of the curtain from the left.*)

RINEHART. Well, that's what happened. I had all the food they left after the party that night, and all winter long whenever I was caught out here in the meadow, I used Grover's burrow as an extra refuge. Now it is February second and I'm on my way to keep my word. He has to get out of that bed. He has too much at stake.

CARLEY. I still say this is all none of your business. Even Grover would agree with that. He doesn't want you for a friend. He said so.

RINEHART. The best kind of friend is one who is on hand whether you want him or not.

CARLEY. You are impossible. All right, go on with it. I'll just wait in the meadow until you have finished with your foolishness.

> (*They exit right and the curtain opens again.* RINE-HART *enters from the right—this time using the back door.* GROVER *is sound asleep with his trophy beside him. The calendar still indicates "last October," and* RINEHART *pulls off the pages until he comes to "this February."*)

RINEHART. Grover! It's time to get up. (GROVER *snores but doesn't move.*) Get up, I say. (*He shakes the cot and* GROVER *pulls the covers over his head.*)

GROVER. Go away.

RINEHART. I won't go away. (*He finds a corn husk on the burrow floor and tickles* GROVER's *feet with it.*)

GROVER. Stop that. I'm ticklish. (*He sits up and we see he is now thin.*)

RINEHART. You are also Groundhog of the Year. Remember that.

GROVER. I don't want to remember that. Wake somebody else.

RINEHART. No use to argue. You were elected. But I can see you've grown thin since October. You need nourishment. Nibble a little corn and you'll be spry as a rabbit.

GROVER. I don't want to be a rabbit. I want to be a hibernating groundhog.

RINEHART. Grover, Punxsutawney is counting on you. The official committee is already on its way out here to watch for your appearance.

GROVER. They can watch until their eyes bug out. What's Punxsutawney to me?

RINEHART. All right, forget Punxsutawney. The groundhogs are counting on you too. Wejack and Otchuck and all the others.

GROVER. What do they care? They're fast asleep.

RINEHART. That's just it. They are confident that you will do your duty and they sleep in peace.

GROVER. Why can't I sleep in peace?

RINEHART. We are going around in circles. You know why. And if you don't do your duty, they'll take away your trophy.

GROVER. OK. (*Reluctantly, he pushes the trophy away from him.*) They can have it.

RINEHART. They will whistle you out of the meadow. You will be alone in the world.

GROVER. I'll go back where I came from. My mother will take me in.

RINEHART. She wouldn't dare. No self-respecting groundhog will have anything to do with you. They won't let
you be a groundhog anymore. They won't even let you
be a woodchuck. Come on, Grover, you must fulfill your
obligation.

GROVER. Look here, Rinehart, you are my friend. You're the
one who insists on that. And if you're my friend you'll
let me go back to sleep. (*He pulls the cover over his
head again.*)

> (RINEHART *paces the burrow. Then with a nod of
> decision he goes to the side of the cot. He is ready
> to tip it over when there is the faint bark of a dog
> offstage left. Instead of tipping over the cot, he sits
> on the edge of it with his head in his hands and
> fingers his long ears.*)

RINEHART. As your true friend I am in this as deep as you
are, Grover. (*He takes* GROVER's *cap and overcoat from
the hook. He folds his ears under the cap, which he pulls
low over his eyes, and dons the coat. Finally he exits
left.*)

GROVER. (*sits up again*) I didn't realize what a fine thing a
friend can be—even one with big ears. (*He settles down
again and there is a moment of quiet.*)

> (RINEHART *reenters hurriedly.*)

RINEHART. I pulled it off, Grover. The committee saw me
and they were satisfied. You are saved. And you can stay

right where you are for six more weeks. I saw my shadow.

GROVER. Thank you, Rinehart. I accept you as a friend. My house is your house.

(*Once again there is the sound of a barking dog offstage left and* CARLEY *enters from the left just as* RINEHART *did in the earlier scene.*)

CARLEY. Whew! That was a close one.

RINEHART. You're making rather free with our front door, aren't you?

CARLEY. Look here, I meant no harm and I'll be eternally grateful. That dog up there is enormous.

GROVER. (*lifts his head and yawns*) I think I've heard this before. Tell him it's all right, Rinehart. He's welcome in our burrow. But for goodness sake keep your voices down. Can't you see someone's sleeping? (*He pulls the cover over his head once more and in a few minutes he is snoring.*)

CARLEY. Rinehart? Is that you, Rinehart?

RINEHART. (*removes the cap*) Of course. And I see you have learned something.

CARLEY. I've certainly learned that an extra burrow here and there isn't a bad thing.

RINEHART. Is that all?

CARLEY. No. You were right. One should grab a friend whenever he can find one and whatever he might be. But what are you doing in that groundhog getup?

RINEHART. Let me tell you, Carley, I have just had the most exciting experience in my life. I have played King of the Weather Prophets, Seer of Seers. The officials of Punxsutawney were all gathered up there in their long coats and mufflers and top hats waiting for me—for *me*. I was the star of the show. Oh, how I wanted to stay there and enjoy it.

CARLEY. Well, you'd gone that far, why didn't you?

RINEHART. The sun was shining, Carley, and when I saw my shadow I remembered why I was there. There will be six more weeks of winter.

CARLEY. What's the matter with you, Rinehart? You know just as well as I do that spring will come when it pleases —when the warm winds blow. It has nothing whatever to do with sun and shadow and Groundhog Day.

RINEHART. Shh—not so loud. Carley Cottontail knows that's true, and Rinehart the Rabbit knows it. Maybe—just maybe—those people in Punxsutawney know it. But they'll never convince us groundhogs.

(*Without bothering to tuck in his ears, he puts* GROVER's *cap back on his head, and as* GROVER *gives one loud snore there is a quick curtain.*)

PRODUCTION NOTES

Any play in which the actors portray animals is a challenge, and *A Groundhog by Any Other Name . . .* is no exception.

The first consideration will be the costuming. You need only to suggest the character—the audience will be cooperative. The groundhogs wear coats, and raincoats will do nicely. If they could all be alike it would be even better. The caps are simply stocking caps, and again as alike as possible.

Grover, who removes his coat, might have an old-fashioned nightshirt under it. After all he plans to retire for the winter. Grover also removes his cap, and perhaps you could make some kind of head-covering, with appropriate ears, out of a fuzzy material. No mask though. You don't want to muffle the dialogue. Incidentally, Grover could put on a nightcap, too, before he heads for his cot. A nightcap is always good for a laugh.

Concentrate on the physical characteristics of the groundhog. He has a way of settling back on his hind legs with his forepaws poised like a begging dog. And give him a habit of moving his head quickly from side to side. It comes from listening for danger. One more thing, the groundhogs are all fat in October, but Grover must come up lean in February. Pillows are in order.

As for the rabbits, they could wear jogging suits or even jeans and T-shirts. Make head-coverings for them too—long ears this time—but remember that Rinehart and Carley are very different characters. Perhaps Rinehart could have much longer ears and wear a vest.

Use whatever facilities you have to create the interior

of the burrow, but with subdued light you might get by with a bare stage. The illusion is all that is necessary. You need a cot, and there might be a table and a couple of chairs, or maybe only a cardboard box or two. If you could make a rock—papier-mâché over a stool—it would be fine. Rinehart could crouch behind it when the groundhogs come in to announce Grover's "election."

The props are minimal. The trophy, the scroll, the picnic baskets, whatever edibles you feel are needed, the corn husk Rinehart finds on the floor, and don't forget the "last October" and "this February" calendar. Check the script. You might want to add other things.

The production can be as elaborate or as simple as you wish, but it will be your enthusiasm for a whimsical weather prophet and a rabbit who drops in uninvited which will allow you to meet the challenge.

ABE LINCOLN:
STAR CENTER

ABE LINCOLN: STAR CENTER

CHARACTERS

STRAD COOPER, A SERIOUS STUDENT AND STAR BASKETBALL
  PLAYER FOR LOCKWOOD JUNIOR HIGH
BENNY, HIS BEST FRIEND, ALSO ON THE TEAM
MISS BERRYMAN, THE DRAMA TEACHER
CHUCK
WILEY
DON   LOCKWOOD STUDENTS AND ALSO BASKETBALL
GIL   PLAYERS
MAC
HOGAN   BASKETBALL PLAYERS AT RIVAL SCHOOL,
CLAY   SOUTHPARK JUNIOR HIGH
OTHER STUDENTS FROM SOUTHPARK, AS MANY AS DESIRED
STUDENT STAGEHANDS AT LOCKWOOD, AS MANY AS DESIRED

SCENE ONE: *A Friday afternoon in the auditorium of Lockwood Junior High School. The curtain is closed—has just
closed on a Lincoln's Day program, a one-student show of
the highlights of the great speeches of the sixteenth president. There is applause from the characters planted in the
audience*—BENNY, CHUCK, WILEY, DON, GIL, *and* MAC—*as*
MISS BERRYMAN, *the drama teacher, comes out from the
right.*

MISS BERRYMAN. (*who is also applauding as she looks offstage to the left, now turns to the audience as she
speaks*) You have been a most attentive student body

audience, and I . . . (*She is drowned out by more applause and she calls to* STRAD *who is in the wings off to the left.*) Strad, I think you'd better come out for a curtain call.

> (STRAD COOPER *enters from the left. He is dressed as Abraham Lincoln in his presidential years—tall stovepipe hat, black suit, black bow tie and, of course, he has a beard.* STRAD *removes his hat and speaks in a deep somber voice.*)

STRAD. I would like to use the words of Abraham Lincoln when he left Springfield for Washington. "To this place, and the kindness of these people, I owe everything." Lincoln was going to the White House when he said that, and I'm just going home, but the words fit. Thank you. (*There is more applause. He bows again, puts his hat back on his head, and exits.*)

MISS BERRYMAN. I know you were impressed with Strad's portrayal of Lincoln and his delivery of the famous speeches. I hope you were also impressed by the philosophy of our sixteenth president. "With malice toward none and charity for all." Those words are equally important in today's world. Well, I certainly didn't intend to make a speech. I think it's about time for the bell. Have a good weekend, and don't forget the basketball game with Southpark tomorrow night. (*She exits right.*)

> (*The characters planted in the audience, who are friends and peers of* STRAD, *get up and head for the*

stage. *Some of them duck under the curtain or go into the wings. Finally, someone opens the curtain, and we see student stagehands clearing away props —a podium perhaps, boxes which had served as a platform with red, white, and blue material still attached to them, and maybe some folding chairs.* STRAD *is sitting alone on a straight chair left center, his bearded chin in his hand.*)

CHUCK. Just let me shake the hand of Abraham Lincoln, fella. You were super.

GIL. "Four score and seven years ago . . ." I liked that one best. Great, Strad, just great.

BENNY. (*standing back a bit, really in awe of his friend*) You were good, real good.

WILEY. How did you ever learn all those speeches?

STRAD. (*in a trancelike voice*) I practiced by reading them out loud. That way I saw the words and heard them at the same time. *He did that.* (STRAD *stands up and strides off the stage in the characteristic gait of Lincoln, coming down on the whole of his foot at once, no heel to toe or toe to heel walk. His friends watch him exit left and then look at each other with puzzled expressions.*)

CHUCK. What's with him?

BENNY. He's still playing Lincoln, I guess.

GIL. They say actors are like that. He'll be Strad Cooper by tomorrow.

WILEY. He'd better be. We sure need him in the game.

(*They all exit right as the curtain falls.*)

SCENE TWO: *In the school yard the next day. Benches are lined up at the back and a few others are arranged haphazardly at center stage. There might be a practice basketball hoop and whatever else is desired to suggest school grounds. The same group of students, except for* BENNY *and* STRAD, *drift in from the left as the curtain opens.*)

WILEY. Did you see those Southpark guys hanging around in front of the school?

CHUCK. Yeah. One of them was Hogan. I didn't know the other. They probably want to watch us practice.

DON. Coach probably won't let them in the gym. But if he did, we'd give them something to worry about.

CHUCK. It's Strad I'm worried about. He's late. Anybody seen him?

WILEY. I didn't even see him last night. He went right home. Said he was busy.

GIL. Did he know Coach wanted a practice today?

DON. I think so. (*looks offstage right*) Here comes Benny. Maybe he's seen him.

> (BENNY *enters from the right looking downcast. He has an old baseball hat on his head and he keeps tugging at the bill.*)

BENNY. If you're talking about Strad, yeah, I've seen him.

WILEY. Is he coming?

BENNY. I don't know. I don't even know whether we can count on him for the game.

CHUCK. What's the matter? Is he sick?

BENNY. Not exactly. (*hesitates*) He's acting strange, and he's still wearing that beard.

DON. You're kidding.

BENNY. Wish I was.

GIL. You mean he didn't take it off all night?

BENNY. Not unless he put it back on this morning. I stopped by his house on my way over here. He was sitting at the breakfast table with a sad mysterious look on his face and that beard.

CHUCK. Didn't his mother say anything?

BENNY. His folks were out last night, and this morning—well, they've got that real estate business and were probably long gone before Strad was out of bed. Besides, you know Mrs. Cooper. A little thing like a crepe hair beard wouldn't bother her. She used to be on the stage herself.

DON. Look, you're his best buddy. Didn't you say anything to him?

BENNY. Tried, but just like yesterday, he got up and walked away. I don't have to be hit on the head.

WILEY. Strad's weird sometimes. He goes all solemn and acts like he has to take care of the whole world.

CHUCK. Maybe he's flipped. Maybe he thinks he is Lincoln.

GIL. Well, he's the best center Lockwood'll ever get. (*looks offstage right*) And you better watch what you say. Here he comes.

> (STRAD *enters right. He is no longer dressed as Lincoln, except for the beard, but he still seems to be playing the part and walks with the same stride of the day before.*)

CHUCK. What's up, Strad. You OK?

WILEY. (*not waiting for* CHUCK *to get an answer*) Didn't you know we're supposed to practice? It's about time you got here.

STRAD. "Nothing valuable can be lost by taking time." First inaugural address, 1861.

DON. Knock it off, Strad. The show's over. Remember we got a big game tonight. (STRAD *heads across the yard to the left exit.*) Hey, where you going?

BENNY. (*who is obviously worried about his friend*) Wait, Strad, I'll walk along. (*They exit together.*)

WILEY. Like I said—weird.

GIL. You're going to have to do something about him.

CHUCK. We might as well leave it to Benny. If anybody can get to Strad, he can.

(MISS BERRYMAN *enters from the right.*)

MAC. (*who hasn't had anything to say until now*) Hi, Miss Berryman. What are you doing at school on a Saturday morning? Don't you get enough of this place during the week?

MISS BERRYMAN. I most certainly do, but that Lincoln costume from yesterday's show has to go back or we'll be charged for the weekend. What's the matter with all of you? You're standing around with such long faces. Who died?

WILEY. It's Strad, and he might as well be dead. He won't even talk to us, and he's still got that Lincoln beard.

MISS BERRYMAN. Is that all?

CHUCK. Isn't that enough?

MISS BERRYMAN. (*laughs*) When the acting bug bites some-body, you can expect most anything. When I was in *Little Women* back in my school days, I wore Meg's clothes for a week. Then the gang planned a bike hike and all those petticoats weren't very practical. It broke the spell. Give him a little time.

DON. We don't have time. We've got a game tonight. Re-member?

MISS BERRYMAN. I see. You're afraid he'll keep it on for the game?

CHUCK. I hope not.

MISS BERRYMAN. Do you really think it matters?

DON. Don't you? It looks dumb. He'll be laughed out of the gym.

WILEY. Those Southpark guys will think it's hilarious.

MISS BERRYMAN. That shouldn't make any difference to Strad. Lincoln looked a little odd to people at times too. He was still wearing homespun pants that didn't come down to his shoe tops when he went into politics. Be-fore his first trip to the Illinois legislature, his friends chipped in and got him a store-bought suit to make him more presentable. No, I don't think laughter will bother Strad.

WILEY. Well, it would bother me.

CHUCK. And it might bother Coach.

MISS BERRYMAN. I see. You think Coach would object?

DON. How would you have felt yesterday if the audience had laughed instead of clapped?

MISS BERRYMAN. I get the point. I'll talk to Strad if I have a chance. And maybe you should ask Coach what he thinks. I still say what difference, though. He's not hurting anybody. I admire someone who has a little spunk and doesn't worry about what people say. To change the subject, will one of you boys take the costume back for me? I'd appreciate it.

GIL. Sure. Come on with me, Mac. They can spare us for awhile.

MISS BERRYMAN. (*as she crosses with* GIL *and* MAC *to the left exit*) I'm sure it will work out. Don't worry. (*She exits with the two boys.*)

WILEY. That's easy enough to say.

CHUCK. I think we ought to see if Coach is here yet. He might have gone right into the gym. (CHUCK, DON, *and* WILEY *exit right as* STRAD *and* BENNY *come back into the yard from the left.*)

STRAD. Benny, I wish you'd quit following me.

BENNY. We been friends for a long time, Strad. I don't care
what you say to anybody else, but I think you should tell
me. What's with this beard? What are you trying to
prove?

STRAD. I'm not trying to prove anything. I don't expect you
to understand.

(*As* STRAD *and* BENNY *talk,* HOGAN *and* CLAY *appear
at the edge of the yard right, but they are not
noticed.*)

BENNY. I'd try to if you'd let me.

STRAD. OK. You know my parents worry about conserva-
tion and cleaning up the air. That's all I hear at home.
They wonder how we're going to preserve this country.
Well, I'm not sure we can, because there's a bigger
problem here.

BENNY. Oh boy, Strad, you're in junior high. Why do you
have to worry about the country? Can't you just worry
about basketball and graduation and maybe getting a
scholarship?

STRAD. I know you guys think I'm crazy, but I had to read
a lot about Lincoln for that show. He was a great man.
Can't you see, Benny, the trouble with this country is
that we don't have any Lincolns anymore—real men who
could deal with anything, who could survive in the

wilderness, build a cabin out of standing trees. Take Wiley—and he's got a lot of good ideas—do you think he could ever make a house out of logs?

BENNY. Of course not. How far do you think he'd get? Every tree in this town belongs to somebody. And as for wilderness, where you going to find that around here? And even if you could find it someplace, you'd have to buy a chunk of it before you could start surviving. There's nothing just for the taking anymore, Strad. You can't even catch a fish without a license.

STRAD. There are other things too. Would Don walk six miles to borrow a book and read by firelight to get an education? Basketball's all he has on his mind.

BENNY. That's the silliest thing you've said yet. We've got schools to go to and libraries. And what's the point in reading by firelight when you can put a hundred-watt bulb in your desk lamp and save your eyes? Besides, what's wrong with basketball?

STRAD. I told you you wouldn't understand. "A man has not time to spend half his life in quarrels."

BENNY. That's another quotation. You don't have to tell me. And you still haven't explained the beard.

STRAD. It makes me feel good. Let it go at that. (*He turns away as though as far as he is concerned the subject is closed.*)

BENNY. How about tonight? Are you going to play?

STRAD. I didn't say I wasn't.

BENNY. The guys are afraid you're going to leave that beard on.

STRAD. What if I am?

BENNY. Darn you, Strad Cooper. You'll be hooted off the floor. Don't you care about . . .

> (BENNY *is interrupted by a commotion just offstage right. The Southpark boys have been listening all this time and now they are being jumped on from behind by* WILEY, CHUCK, *and* DON. *The impact pushes them onto the stage.*)

HOGAN. OK. Lay off. There's no law that says we can't be here. It's public property.

CHUCK. Well, we don't like anybody creeping around. Beat it. We'll see you tonight.

CLAY. We thought we'd hang around and watch you practice.

WILEY. Well, we aren't practicing. Besides, watching us practice is one thing. Listening in on private conversations is another.

HOGAN. We heard enough anyhow. (*He laughs.*) Our team will be happy to know they're playing Old Honest Abe tonight. We'll be around. (CHUCK *and* DON *push the boys offstage right.*)

WILEY. (*to* STRAD) You sure aren't going to play like that, are you?

STRAD. Why not?

DON. What if Coach says you can't?

STRAD. "We won't jump that ditch until we come to it."

BENNY. There you go again using Lincoln's words. I wish you'd quit that.

STRAD. There's nothing wrong with Lincoln's words.

WILEY. I don't mind telling you they're making me sick.

(COACH *enters from the right.*)

COACH. Hey, what's been going on around here? I saw the Southpark fellows outside—*and* Miss Berryman.

BENNY. Then you know what's been going on.

COACH. Yes, I guess I do. That was a terrific show yesterday, Strad. Congratulations. But this is another day. How about it? What if I said take that makeup off or you don't play tonight?

STRAD. (*thoughtfully*) Then I guess I wouldn't play.

COACH. The truth is I don't really care. Miss Berryman says you are expressing your individualism. That's important. She says too, that you have some kind of personal commitment to Lincoln. That's all right too, I guess. But you know Hogan and that other fellow will stir up a lot of gaff. People will think it's funny, Strad. It's human nature. The rest of the team—and maybe the student body—might object.

WILEY. Well, I object. We're a good team, and I don't want to be laughed at. This is an important game.

DON. I don't either. If Strad leaves that dumb thing on his face, count me out.

WILEY. Goes for me too.

COACH. How about you, Benny?

BENNY. Oh, I'd play, but I'm not exactly the team's most important player.

CHUCK. I'd play too, but I wouldn't like it.

COACH. Then this is about the way it stands. I have two choices. Tell you, Strad, that you can't play with the beard and lose my best center. Let you play with the beard and lose my two forwards. Either way it may cost us the game. The only thing I can say is think about it, all of you. Tell Gil and Mac they might as well stand by. I may need them. And I guess we'll just cancel the practice. (WILEY, DON, *and* CHUCK *head for the left exit.*)

BENNY. (*calling after them*) Wait, you guys. Let's talk about it. (BENNY *exits with the three fellows and* STRAD *starts off right alone.*)

COACH. (*calls him back*) Hold on a second, Strad. Miss Berryman tried to explain to me about this fascination you have with Lincoln. I admit I don't understand it. Don't you care about your school? Don't you care about the rest of the team? Or me?

STRAD. You sound like Benny.

COACH. There's something else. You may lose the chance at a scholarship. Isn't that important to you?

STRAD. Everybody makes such a big thing of this, Coach. What difference does this beard make? It's just makeup.

COACH. That's it. You said it. What difference does it make? Why should it matter to you to keep it on?

STRAD. It just does. It makes me feel that sometime, somehow, I could be a little bit like Lincoln. I know that sounds dumb, because, of course, I can't keep it on forever. I know you don't understand.

COACH. Lincoln lived in his world—and that was over a hundred years ago—and you have to live in yours. It's what's inside you that would make you a Lincoln. I hope you change your mind, Strad, but I'm going to have a team tonight, one way or the other. Sorry. (*He exits left and* STRAD *sits back down on the bench. He is alone with a long sad face as* MISS BERRYMAN *enters right.*)

MISS BERRYMAN. Strad! (*He turns toward her and gets to his feet.*) I told Benny and the others how I feel about your Lincoln makeup.

STRAD. That you think it's silly?

MISS BERRYMAN. No, not at all. Quite the contrary. But in all fairness, I think I should talk to you not about the beard but about Lincoln the man. You presented the president of the war years, and you studied about his early life—all the hardships and the loss of four people he loved, his mother, the girl he was going to marry, and two sons.

STRAD. That's just it. Everything was hard for him. That's why he made something of his life. Everything is so easy now.

MISS BERRYMAN. That's strange for a boy your age to be saying that. And frankly I think life is just as hard today. What chance would you have, for example, to become a lawyer simply by reading books? Lincoln was great not because of his hardships, but in spite of them. He had a mind and a character to match his stature. Don't you think he would have been just as great if he'd been able to go to school?

STRAD. I hadn't thought about that.

MISS BERRYMAN. He was a boy who liked fun and laughter and people, and he wasn't all that fond of manual labor. Maybe that's why he turned to books. You know, Strad, it isn't easier now, it's just different. There can be a Lincoln in the future—a man or woman of honesty and principle and commitment.

STRAD. What are you trying to tell me, Miss Berryman, that I ought to take off this makeup and play tonight? Well, it's too late. I told Coach I wouldn't.

MISS BERRYMAN. I don't think that's really what I had in mind. I think I wanted to remind you of Lincoln's qualities, of his compassion for others, of his good common sense. If you're going to be a Lincoln, be the whole man. (*She exits right and* STRAD *walks somberly offstage left as the curtain falls.*)

SCENE THREE: *In the school yard an hour before the game.* CHUCK, MAC, GIL, WILEY, *and* DON *enter from the left.*)

WILEY. Coach told me Strad wasn't playing so I guess Don and I are. Are you starting center, Mac?

MAC. I don't know yet.

DON. Where's Benny?

GIL. With Strad I suppose—trying to talk some sense into him. Probably been with him all afternoon.

CHUCK. Not all afternoon. My sister saw Benny at the library about four o'clock. She said he had about a hundred books piled up in front of him. Crazy way to spend a Saturday. (STRAD *enters right with* BENNY *on his heels.*)

STRAD. You might as well give up, Benny. It's all settled.
Mac's in the game. I'm out. But that doesn't mean I don't
want the team to win. Like Lincoln said . . .

(*There is a commotion offstage right, and* HOGAN
and CLAY *with a crowd of other Southpark students
enter. They are all dressed as Abraham Lincoln,
makeshift though the costumes are, and they all
wear beards. Some students carry banners—*"Hurrah
for Southpark," "Abe Lincoln, Star Center," "Sorry,
Mr. Lincoln," *and there is a good deal of shouting
for victory over Lockwood.*)

HOGAN. Hey, you guys, get ready for battle, and this time
the south will win—Southpark that is.

(*The Lockwood boys have been taken by surprise
and they are speechless for a few moments. Then*
STRAD *speaks.*)

STRAD. Benny! They're making fun of Abraham Lincoln!

BENNY. Not Lincoln, Strad, you. Our whole team.

CLAY. Lincoln was a great president, but he's dead! And
Lockwood'll be dead too after tonight.

(*They march around the stage jeering and waving
their banners, and now the Lockwood boys shout
back—*"That's what you say," "Go on back where
you came from, under the rocks." "Who says?")

HOGAN. We'll see you in the gym. Be ready to surrender.

(*The Southpark students exit left and* HOGAN *is about to follow, but* STRAD, *who is furious, pulls him back and they wrestle with each other as the others watch.*)

BENNY. You started something you can't finish, Hogan. Lincoln was a wrestler too. Come on, Strad!

CHUCK. That's right. Come on!

(*After a few minutes of struggle,* HOGAN *breaks away and exits left.* STRAD *gets up off the ground. He is bedraggled and the beard is half gone.*)

CHUCK. Don't worry, Strad, we'll beat those guys for you tonight.

STRAD. They didn't have to take it out on you guys.

BENNY. What did you expect? We been trying to tell you they'd make fun of us. Look here, you've been throwing Lincoln at me all day. Well, I looked up a few things myself—only I can't remember like you can so I wrote them down. (*He pulls off his cap and takes a paper from it.*) You know Lincoln kept stuff in his hat. Notes, letters, ideas. Well, here's something you can put in your hat. (*He reads from the paper.*) "A house divided against itself cannot stand." That wasn't a saying he made up himself, but he knew it was true. Can't you see you divided us, pulled our team all apart just on account of that old beard?

STRAD. I'm sorry.

BENNY. If you were really sorry, you'd do something about it.

STRAD. I'm staying out of the game. (*He walks downstage left away from the others.*) I won't even come to watch if it'll help.

BENNY. What good do you think that'll do? Look, you're so hung up on Lincoln, but you forget he liked a good joke and he needed to laugh. (*He takes another paper from his cap.*) You even said this in your show yesterday. Remember? How after the Battle of Fredericksburg it was going real bad in the war and he sort of took time out to read some funny stories by a guy named Artemus Ward. People thought there was something wrong with Lincoln because he did that. But he said . . .

STRAD. (*who has obviously been thinking over the whole situation now interrupts*) I know, he said if he didn't have that comic stuff to read his heart would break.

BENNY. Why can't you just laugh at Hogan's joke? (STRAD *turns back to* BENNY *and* BENNY, *seeing the makeup half hanging, laughs.*) You sure do look silly in that beard, especially now that it's half gone.

STRAD. (*pulls at the beard and suddenly breaks out in laughter too*) You know when Hogan got ahold of it I thought I was going to lose my chin. You win. United we stand. Get the stuff from Miss Berryman to take this thing off, and let's get ready for a game. How about it, Mac? That'll mean you won't start at center. Is that OK?

MAC. You never really left the team. (*laughs*) But I'll stand by in case John Wilkes Booth shows up in the crowd.

CHUCK. I'll go see Miss Berryman. (*He exits left.*)

GIL. Come on, Mac, we'll go tell Coach. (*He and* MAC *exit left.*)

DON. Thanks, Strad.

WILEY. We're going to win for sure now.

(DON *and* WILEY *exit left and* STRAD *and* BENNY *are alone.*)

BENNY. You know, Strad, I'll bet Abe Lincoln's out there someplace wishing he was in your shoes.

STRAD. Why do you say that?

BENNY. He was six-foot-four, for Pete's sake, and his hands were *big*. I think he'd like being the star center.

(*quick curtain*)

PRODUCTION NOTES

Scene One of *Abe Lincoln: Star Center* is tricky. The audience may not be prepared for a play that opens with lines which seem to indicate the show is over. If you have a printed program this could be made clear in black and white. Or perhaps you can have someone introduce the play and explain the situation. Otherwise the success of the gimmick will be in the hands of your characters.

Make sure the announcement about the basketball game with Southpark comes out loud and clear and the message will be conveyed that this is make-believe—that you are presenting a play. You might also have trouble when the characters planted in the audience get up from their places and go onto the stage. Others might start to follow suit. Don't let this happen. Put the six boys in the same row, or as a last resort have them tell the people around them that they are members of the cast, a part of the show. One way or another you will manage the opening, and as soon as the curtain goes up everything should be clear.

Scenes Two and Three take place in the school yard and require very little in the way of a set. There is, however, virtually no time for preparation. The benches along the back could, of course, be on the stage from the beginning, and why not let the student stagehands in Scene One arrange the other benches and bring on the practice hoop and whatever else you want. It will appear as though they are setting up for some later program. No one will pay any attention to what they are doing as long as they do it quietly. It would be fine to have a backdrop for Scenes Two and Three which pictures a brick building or a view of school grounds, something to give the illusion of being at Lockwood Junior High.

The foregoing suggestions for staging are given with the assumption that you have a stage and a curtain. If you have more limited facilities, you will have to rely on someone introducing the show and explaining whatever is necessary.

There is some good physical action in the play—first in the opening scene, later on with the arrival of Hogan and Clay, and still later with the harassment by the Southpark students and the fight—but there is still a lot of "talk." You will want to strive for incidental movement as well. Strad might pace about with Benny at his heels during their first long scene together. At other times the boys can practice with the ball, especially if there is a hoop on stage. Boys seldom stand still anyhow. A director will have further ideas.

The props needed are minimal—basketballs, of course, the banners Hogan and his gang bring in, for which you can use newsprint or cardboard, and the papers Benny puts in his cap. It might be fun for the Southpark boys to have a Confederate flag. Maybe they could make one. That's about all except for the red, white, and blue draped boxes and the podium in Scene One. Perhaps they should be considered as part of the set, but in any event, don't forget them.

As for the costumes, Strad's Lincoln outfit is the only one really described in the script. Be as faithful to that as you can. Raid the attic, visit the local costume shop, or get someone who is handy with a needle. Lincoln should be Lincoln up to his stovepipe hat, which in a pinch could be fashioned of cardboard. But it is the beard which must be authentic. It is the crux of the whole play. The South-park boys are Lincolns too, but their costumes can be—should be—makeshift. They have come to mock. They may have only portions of the Lincoln dress as long as they have some kind of beard. The hook-on kind, even the rubbed-on-with-charcoal kind, would suffice. There won't be enough time for anything realistic anyhow.

Miss Berryman is a teacher. The time is now. She would wear whatever is appropriate for your community. The same is true of the Coach and the boys. Whatever they wear in Scene One will do for Scene Two. There is time for all but Strad, and possibly Benny, to put on sweat suits for Scene Three if they have them. It is optional. Benny's cap is important. Why not make it a characteristic of Benny to wear that cap wherever he goes. His trademark.

Some attention must be given to casting. Strad is a basketball center. He will be the tallest boy around. And Benny, who is a little shy and says he isn't the team's most important player, will be considerably smaller than his best friend. Do develop characteristics for the other boys, making each one different. Mac is quiet; Wiley and Don on the obstinate side—say they won't play if Strad wears the beard; Gil seems to be easy going; and Chuck is apparently the leader.

Although Strad Cooper's hero worship took an unusual turn, *Abe Lincoln: Star Center* is intended as a reminder that our sixteenth president was indeed a great man.

THE BIG RED HEART

THE BIG RED HEART

CHARACTERS

TIP CONROY, A BOY OF TODAY
IRMA CONROY, HIS OLDER SISTER
BARBARA CONROY, A YOUNGER SISTER
KENNY, TIP'S FRIEND
GRIMSLEY, THE "BABY-SITTER"
BRIAN, IRMA'S BOYFRIEND

The scene is laid in the living room of the Conroy home. The exit to the outside is on the right, and the one to the rest of the house is on the left. At center back there is a fireplace with a mantel, and at left center, perhaps in front of a davenport there is a coffee table. Other furnishings are optional and whatever is needed to make a comfortable, contemporary room.

As the curtain opens, the doorbell is ringing and TIP *hurries in from the left to answer it. His friend,* KENNY, *enters, carrying a large white envelope which is bordered in red.*

TIP. Hi. Whatcha got?

KENNY. A valentine, I guess.

TIP. Don't you know? Where did you get it? From that new girl? The pretty one? Little old Debra? (*He laughs.*)

KENNY. (*defensively*) No, it's not from little old Debra. She has her eye on you anyhow. If you'll keep still I'll

tell you where I got it. It was on your front porch—
just leaning up against the door. There isn't any name
on it.

TIP. Open it.

KENNY. You open it. It was leaning up against your door.

(TIP *opens the envelope and takes out a big red paper heart, elaborately decorated with lace and
ribbons.*)

TIP. (*holding it up*) Look at this! (*He opens it up and
reads the words inside.*) "To My Valentine." There's no
name anywhere.

KENNY. Who do you suppose it's for?

TIP. Not me, that's sure. Who do you suppose it's from?
Who'd give anybody this kind of a dumb thing?

KENNY. I wonder how long it's been out on your porch.
Must not have been there when you came home.

TIP. Grimsley makes us use the back door. It could have
been there all day.

KENNY. (*inspecting the valentine*) Who's Grisley?

TIP. Not Grisley, dope—Grimsley. The baby-sitter.

KENNY. (*mocking*) You got a baby-sitter?

TIP. Well, you know, for Barb. Anyhow she's staying here this week while mom and dad are away.

KENNY. OK. Grimsley. Still sounds like a bear.

GRIMSLEY. (*from offstage left in a harsh, demanding voice*) Tip Conroy! Don't forget I expect you to have the wastebaskets emptied and the trash out in the alley before dinner.

TIP. (*waggling his thumb toward the sound of the voice*) More like a lion. (*answers* GRIMSLEY) Don't worry, I'll do it. (*back to* KENNY) Mom got her at some agency—told us to be nice to her because she's all alone in the world. I say, no wonder. Anyhow Grimsley's her name and that's what she wants us to call her. It's all right with me.

> (*There are sounds offstage right and* BARBARA *dashes in, shouting over her shoulder to someone outside.*)

BARBARA. After this you keep your hands off my valentines.

TIP. Hey! That's the front door you're using. How come you forgot Grimsley's rule?

BARBARA. I was in a hurry. I had to get away from that creepy Peter. (*She puts her books and a pile of valentines on the coffee table and goes back to shout again at Peter.*) You're just mad because you didn't get any.

TIP. (*who has picked up one of* BARBARA's *valentines, now reads it*) "Please don't be my valentine—you look just like a clown. Your feet are pointing backwards, and your head's on upside down." That's a good one, Barb. Custom made for you. Who's it from?

BARBARA. None of your business, Tip Conroy, and you let my things alone too.

TIP. Yah. Don't be so touchy. I was only kidding.

KENNY. (*to* TIP) Maybe the big heart's hers. (*He hands* BARBARA *the fancy valentine.*) You think somebody left this on the front porch for you, Barb? It's kind of pretty.

BARBARA. (*looking it over*) I don't know anybody who gives pretty valentines. Everybody in my class has to be funny. (*She hands the valentine to* TIP *who puts it down on a convenient chair as* GRIMSLEY *enters from the left.*)

GRIMSLEY. I see you're finally home, Barbara. It's about time. (*She nods toward* KENNY.) And who's this boy?

KENNY. I'm Kenny, ma'am.

TIP. He's my friend, Grimsley. He lives just a couple of houses down the street.

GRIMSLEY. (*rather curtly*) Nice to have a friend so close I suppose. (*She goes right on, turning her attention to the pile of valentines on the table.*) And what's this clutter all over the table? (*She picks up a few of the valentines.*)

BARBARA. My valentines. I got them at school today.

GRIMSLEY. (*reading the one she has been looking at*) "A spider is a scary thing; a horny toad is too, But a housefly's just a pesky pest—Like you." How disgusting! You call this a valentine? (*She thumbs through a few more without reading them aloud.*) A valentine should be a thing of beauty, and the sentiment endearing.

TIP. Mushy, you mean.

GRIMSLEY. Nothing of the sort. Touching, sincere, heart-warming.

TIP. I'd be embarrassed to give anything heartwarming.

KENNY. I don't know anybody who'd send anything like that.

GRIMSLEY. It doesn't always matter whether you know who sent it. You are supposed to wonder.

BARBARA. I don't care who mine are from. They're all yucky.

GRIMSLEY. (*goes on as though* BARBARA *hadn't spoken*) And the best ones are those that seem to appear out of nowhere for people who need them.

KENNY. Need them? Who needs a valentine?

GRIMSLEY. You might be surprised, my boy. The discouraged, the lonely, the disheartened. And a really fine valentine has a magic about it.

TIP. Magic? You mean like it could change somebody into something he isn't? Watch out, Barb. You might wake up in the morning—a fly.

GRIMSLEY. (*almost as though she has been talking to herself*) A different kind of magic, like a velvet touch. But it could change a person, I suppose. Yes, it could. (*Then she directs a question to them all.*) Have you never seen a valentine like that?

BARBARA. (*bringing the conversation back to the commonplace*) One thing sure, nobody gives me that kind.

GRIMSLEY. Perhaps people should remember how the custom began. Valentine was in prison you know, and he sent a greeting to the jailer's daughter because she'd been kind to him. He signed it, "Your Valentine."

BARBARA. My teacher says no one really knows whether that's true or not.

GRIMSLEY. It's better to believe that story than to let Valentine's Day come to this sort of thing. (*She indicates* BARBARA's *collection. Then suddenly she changes the subject.*) Well, enough chatter. You have chores to do too, Barbara, and you can start with putting these away. (*indicates the valentines again and then turns abruptly on her heel and exits left*)

KENNY. You should have shown Grimsley the red heart.

TIP. I thought of it, but it can't be hers. We'd just get another long speech.

KENNY. Maybe it's for your mom.

TIP. Kenny, you are so dense. Mom and dad are out of town. That's why Grimsley's here. It's probably Irma's.

(IRMA *enters from the left in time to hear her name.*)

IRMA. What's mine?

TIP. (*hands the valentine to* IRMA) This. It was on the front porch. And I said "probably." We don't know. There's no name on it.

IRMA. (*takes the valentine and admires it*) Hmmm. I haven't had anything from Brian yet. Of course it's mine. (*She starts off with it.*)

TIP. Wait a minute. Check it out. If it isn't yours, bring it back. We may have a mystery on our hands.

IRMA. (*calling out as she exits left*) Don't worry, I will.
(IRMA *is no sooner out of the room than the doorbell
rings.* BARBARA *answers it and* BRIAN *enters.*)

BARBARA. Hi, Brian. We were just talking about you—
that is, Irma was.

TIP. (*shouts for* IRMA) Hey, Irma, the Valentine Kid is
here. (IRMA *enters from the left.*)

BRIAN. What's with this "Valentine Kid"?

IRMA. I got your valentine, Brian, and thanks. (*She shows
him the red heart.*) Where in the world did you find
such a fancy one?

TIP. (*teasing*) Maybe he made it. (*laughs*)

BRIAN. (*embarrassed*) That isn't from me. Valentines are
silly anyhow. How about going for a root beer?

IRMA. Great. (*She tosses the valentine on the table.*) There
you are—returned. I'd rather have a root beer any day.

GRIMSLEY. (*from offstage left*) Irma! If that's Brian Dud-
ley, you are not going anywhere until your room is clean
—and I mean *clean.* Do you hear me?

IRMA. (*calling to* GRIMSLEY) Yes, I hear you. (*to* BRIAN)
See you later.

BRIAN. OK. Boy, I'll bet you'll be glad when your folks get back. (*He exits right.*)

TIP. Anyhow, that takes care of the valentine as far as Irma's concerned. If it's not from Brian, it's not Irma's.

IRMA. (*defensively*) I don't know about that. But no, it isn't mine.

KENNY. Maybe it *is* for Grimsley. It's sure one of those fancy things she was talking about.

IRMA. Grimsley was talking about valentines?

BARBARA. She thinks they're magic—some of them anyhow.

IRMA. I'd like one with magic enough to clean that room of mine. But how come you didn't ask her right then if it was hers?

TIP. Are you kidding? Maybe a hundred years ago she got these goopy things, but not now.

KENNY. Maybe she's one of the "discouraged and disheartened."

IRMA. You have to be fair. She is a good cook.

TIP. True.

BARBARA. Super chocolate pie.

KENNY. If she bakes chocolate chip cookies too, she can be my valentine.

IRMA. We might as well ask her. We're running out of candidates.

BARBARA. I'll go get her. (BARBARA *exits left.*)

KENNY. If it isn't Grimsley's either, maybe the guy left it at the wrong house.

IRMA. You'd think he'd know where his valentine lived.

TIP. I'm not sure about that. Anybody dumb enough to give a thing like this just might be dumb enough not to know where he's going. Of course, we don't even know it's a guy.

GRIMSLEY. (GRIMSLEY *hurries in from the left with* BARBARA. *She is fussing with* BARBARA's *hair.*) I don't know why you can't learn to keep your hair looking neat. (*Then she turns her attention to* TIP *and* IRMA.) This had better be important. I'm busy in the kitchen. Too many interruptions and there won't be any dinner.

IRMA. There's something we want to ask you, Grimsley.

GRIMSLEY. Go ahead, but don't waste time.

TIP. Well, this valentine was sort of left on the porch. It doesn't belong to any of us. We wondered if . . . (*He holds it out for her to see.*)

GRIMSLEY. (*Looks startled. Gradually an expression of warmth comes over her face and she smiles.*) Why yes, yes, of course. (*She takes the valentine, fingers the lace, and her voice becomes soft.*) Thank you. It's lovelier than usual. Thank you very much.

TIP. (*in surprise*) It is yours? Well, sorry that we opened it. There wasn't any name and . . .

GRIMSLEY. That's quite all right. (*She stands admiring the big red heart for a moment.*) Remember what I told you—a thing of beauty? Now this is what I call a valentine. (*She takes it to the mantel and sets it up in a place of prominence.*) But it is something to be shared. I'll leave it right here for everyone to see and enjoy. Now I'd better get back to the kitchen. (*She turns abruptly to* TIP.) And Tip, would you like to have Kenny stay for dinner? There's plenty of food.

TIP. Well, gee, sure. Want to, Kenny?

KENNY. Yeah. Great. Thanks.

GRIMSLEY. Just go ask your mother and hurry back. (*She exits left.*)

TIP. How about that? What happened to the lion?

IRMA. I don't believe it. She's been so grouchy.

KENNY. Maybe the valentine did it.

BARBARA. She said a valentine could change a person. Boy, she sure changed.

IRMA. What did she mean though—it was "lovelier than usual"? Almost as though she expected it. Did she tell you she usually gets a fancy valentine like this?

TIP. No, she didn't, and I think she just meant it was prettier than those she was talking to us about.

KENNY. At least the big red heart's been claimed. I'd better go home and ask mom about dinner.

TIP. Yeah. Before the magic wears off and Grimsley changes her mind.

KENNY. She won't change her mind. Not now. (KENNY *exits right*.)

TIP. I'd better take care of the trash. (*exits left*)

IRMA. And I ought to at least start on my room. I don't want to break the spell.

BARBARA. I'll help you if you'll help me.

IRMA. OK. I'll get the cleaning stuff. You can start picking up these things. (*She indicates the books and valentines and then exits left.*)

BARBARA. (*Left alone with the valentine, she goes to look at it more closely and now speaks to herself.*) It is pretty, and it does look handmade. Next year I think I'll try to make some like it.

> (TIP, *coming from one of the other rooms with a wastebasket in hand, enters from the left as* BARBARA *is speaking.*)

TIP. I guess it's all right, Barb, if you like that sort of thing. Yeah, it's all right.

BARBARA. I wonder who sent it to her.

TIP. I wonder if she knows.

BARBARA. Tip, there wasn't any name on it. How could she be so sure it was hers? And how can we be sure?

> (IRMA *comes in from the left with a broom, dustpan, and a can of spray cleaner in time to hear* BARBARA'S *last remark.*)

IRMA. Are we sure? I've been thinking about it. I don't believe the valentine is Grimsley's.

TIP. Maybe you're right.

IRMA. Mom said she was all alone in the world. That means no husband, no children, no family at all.

TIP. And who else but family would send Grimsley a valentine? Especially at our house. She's only here for a few days.

BARBARA. Maybe she has a boyfriend.

TIP. Grimsley?

BARBARA. Well, maybe other friends who know she's staying here. Maybe she gets valentines from the kids she baby-sits with. Maybe that's why she said this one was lovelier than usual.

IRMA. That's a lot of maybe. We're just talking around in circles, but you did hit on something, Barb. I'll bet she thinks we gave it to her.

TIP. She did overthank us.

IRMA. And she left it on the mantle for all to enjoy. That's just what she said.

BARBARA. Are we going to let her know it isn't from us?

TIP. We could ask her who sent it to her. That would tell her we weren't the ones.

IRMA. Not necessarily, and I think we ought to let well enough alone.

BARBARA. I do too. So we did our good deed for the week—even if we didn't.

TIP. But if she accepted it because she thought it was from us, we're right back where we started. Who does it belong to, and who left it on the porch?

IRMA. We all refused it—said it wasn't ours, but it could belong to one of us after all. You know, Tip, that new girl, Debra Sykes? She told me she liked you. She could have put it on the porch hoping you would know it was for you.

TIP. (*obviously pleased but trying to cover it up*) I was thinking it could be yours, Barbara. Peter did follow you home. Maybe he wanted to see if the valentine had been taken in. He sure wouldn't own up to giving it to you.

BARBARA. I think you're both wrong. Irma, you saw how red in the face Brian got when you thanked him for the valentine in front of everybody. Especially after Tip made that crack about making it himself. I bet it's from him after all.

IRMA. I guess now we'll never know. Well, Grimsley said you were supposed to wonder.

(GRIMSLEY *enters from the left.*)

GRIMSLEY. Your friend not back yet? Dinner's about ready, and I see you've barely started on your work. Well, if you don't finish now, you can do it later. (TIP, IRMA, *and* BARBARA *exchange significant looks of disbelief at* GRIMSLEY's *transformation. Then they exit left with promises that they will hurry.* GRIMSLEY *is left alone with the valentine. She stands admiring it when there is a knock at the door and* KENNY, *not waiting to be admitted, enters excitedly.*)

KENNY. It's all right, ma'am, I can stay. Sorry I was so long. I told my mother what you said about valentines, and you know she said that was funny, because when she was a little girl a real fancy one was left in their mailbox. No name on it—just like this one. (*He indicates the red heart on the mantel.*) They had just moved into a new town and didn't know anybody. Weird, mom said.

GRIMSLEY. It was Valentine's Day, Kenny.

KENNY. Mom said they never did find out who it was from —or who it was for. I'm not sure I like mysteries like that. I'm glad the red heart was yours.

GRIMSLEY. You only took my word for that, Kenny. I think Barbara and Irma and Tip aren't so certain. Still, we are in this together, and it could be mine.

KENNY. You really don't know who it came from then? Who delivered it?

GRIMSLEY. Does it matter? (*changes the subject*) Tip is emptying the wastebaskets, Kenny. Go help him and then tell them all to come to dinner. (*as* KENNY *gets to the left exit, she adds*) Remember, the best ones are those that seem to appear out of nowhere.

KENNY. If you say so, ma'am. (*He exits.*)

GRIMSLEY. (*now alone in the room, moves to center stage and finishes her sentence*) And come to the ones who need them. Yes, it could be mine. (*She exits left and a spotlight settles on the valentine and holds as the curtain falls.*)

PRODUCTION NOTES

As far as props, costumes, and set requirements are concerned, *The Big Red Heart* is probably the easiest of plays to produce. All the action takes place in a comfortably furnished, contemporary living room. If it is difficult to provide a fireplace with a mantel, something else might be substituted—a high bookcase perhaps—on which the fancy valentine can be displayed to advantage. There is mention of a doorbell, but a good loud knock will suffice. In fact, on Kenny's second entrance, the script calls for him to knock.

Characters wear whatever is currently in fashion, but Grimsley might be an eccentric. Why not make her severe-looking, dressed in a dark skirt and tailored blouse, with her hair pulled back in a bun? Then when the valentine "changes" her, there could be a softening of her appearance. A bit of this could happen right before the eyes of the audience. She could put a hand to her hair and almost unconsciously pull some of the tight strands from their mooring. Along with the modulation of her voice you will have evidence of change. When she comes back on the stage after an exit, that change will be more pronounced. Her hairstyle can be different and the sleeves of her blouse turned back in a more casual way.

Check through the script for props. There are the books that Barbara brings home, the wastebasket that Tip carries in, the cleaning equipment for Irma. And, of course, the big red heart. Do come up with something impressive. It must be unusually large, bright red, and heavy on the lace and ribbons. Also remember the white envelope is bordered in red.

Even though the use of the spotlight on the red heart would be effective, there can be an alternative to the ending. After Grimsley's last line and her exit, the stage can simply remain empty for a moment. The audience will be aware that the valentine is significant. It dominates the stage as the curtain falls.

Since you will have so little problem with *The Big Red Heart* from a physical standpoint, devote time and effort to the mystical aspects of the play. Develop Grimsley as one who understands that the best valentines are those which seem to appear out of nowhere and Kenny as a sensitive boy who finds kinship with Grimsley even though he isn't sure he likes mysteries.

The questions in the play remain unanswered. They are provocative—open to speculation. As Grimsley says, "You are supposed to wonder."

MISS LACEY AND
THE PRESIDENT

MISS LACEY AND THE PRESIDENT

CHARACTERS

SUE ELLA, A YOUNG GIRL WITH HEART

PATCH, HER FRIEND

MISS LACEY CULPEPPER, AN ELDERLY INDIVIDUALIST

THE YOUNG MISS LACEY, SIX YEARS OLD

MRS. BLAZER, THE SOCIAL SERVICE REPRESENTATIVE

MR. STIMSON, FROM THE COUNTY MUSEUM

MR. GATES, OF BOXBY AND GATES, LEGAL COUNSELORS

GEORGE WASHINGTON, TWELVE YEARS OLD

The time is February twenty-second, and as the play begins SUE ELLA *and* PATCH, *dressed for the nippy end-of-winter weather, enter left in front of the closed curtain.* SUE ELLA *is in the lead and in a hurry.*

SUE ELLA. Hurry up, Patch, if you're coming with me.

PATCH. I don't see why you want to waste time out there with Miss Lacey, Sue Ella. You know she's crazy as a coot.

SUE ELLA. I don't know any such thing. If it hadn't been for Miss Lacey and those books of hers, I'd have flunked American History last year for sure. She's just an individualist. Besides, it's her birthday. George Washington and Miss Lacey Culpepper both born on the twenty-second of February. I think that's special. You don't have to come if you don't want to.

PATCH. Oh, I'll come. But my brother says she *talks* to George Washington, and in my book that's crazy.

(*They exit right as the curtain opens on the scene in front of Miss Lacey Culpepper's house, which is at center back. We need to see only a facade of the house. The front door, providing an exit, is flanked by two windows with shades and curtains. The kitchen window is to the right of the door, and we can see a blackened metal cup and perhaps a potted plant on the sill. The living room window is on the left. The low porch is elevated by only a couple of steps, and under the left window there is a large trunk or chest.* MISS LACEY, *enveloped in a heavy coat and wearing a floppy hat tied on with a bright-colored scarf, is putting up the flag on the porch post at the right of the steps. When she finishes the task, she goes down into the yard and stands admiring it for a moment before she speaks.*)

MISS LACEY. There it is, Mr. President, George Washington, sir. A lot more stars in it now, but it's still your flag and mine. A happy birthday to the two of us. Of course, you don't really have birthdays any more, and I don't need them. Still, one year just seems to slide into the next, and I guess I'll stay around until you come to see me. Maybe you could help me find the box.

(*There is the sound of an approaching car offstage left—perhaps a squeal of brakes. The aura of fantasy is gone, and* MISS LACEY *looks in the direction of the noise. Then she bustles into the house, pulls down the window shades and comes out again, closing the front door behind her. This business taken care of, she proceeds to climb into the trunk to hide as* MR. STIMSON, *neatly dressed and wearing a topcoat and hat, enters from the left. He goes to the door and knocks. When there is no response, he raps on the windows and then calls out.*)

MR. STIMSON. Anyone here? (*When he receives no answer, he comes down off the porch, and at that moment* MRS. BLAZER, *also dressed for the cold, enters left.* MR. STIMSON *approaches her.*) Miss Culpepper?

MRS. BLAZER. Goodness no. I've come to see her myself. But if she's spotted us, I'm sure she won't appear. It's happened before. As a matter of fact, I've yet to meet the lady.

MR. STIMSON. You might be able to give me some information. I'm from the County Museum. (*He hands her a card.*) We've had a lead—I don't know how reliable— that Miss Culpepper might have something for our Washington collection. I happened to be in the area and, holiday or no, I thought I'd check it out. No more appropriate day, I guess. I hope it's not a wild goose chase. I'll know when I see Miss Culpepper.

MRS. BLAZER. If you see her. (*She goes onto the porch and calls out as she knocks.*) Miss Culpepper, I wish you wouldn't hide when I come. I need to talk to you. I only want to help. (*She goes to the windows, too, but gets no response.*)

MR. STIMSON. Maybe she really isn't here.

MRS. BLAZER. Oh, I think she's here all right. (*She speaks to* MISS LACEY *again—louder.*) If you don't want to talk to me, Miss Culpepper, perhaps you'll see Mr. Gates when he comes. (*She turns to* MR. STIMSON *and comes down off the porch as she looks at the card in her hand. The lid of the trunk is raised slightly and* MISS LACEY *peeks out, but neither* MR. STIMSON *nor* MRS. BLAZER *sees her.*) Good luck with your lead, Mr. Stimson, but I wouldn't count on Lacey Culpepper having anything of historical value. No one has mentioned the possibility to me, and even though I haven't seen her or the inside of her house, I've been well informed. Her family goes back far enough, I guess. In fact, I've heard one of her ancestors was with Washington at Valley Forge, but nobody seems to think there's any truth to that. (*She gets back to the issue at hand.*) I guess I might as well give up for the moment. Mr. Gates told me she'd be like this.

MR. STIMSON. She's eccentric, I take it.

MRS. BLAZER. More than that, I'm afraid. The report we had was that she shouldn't be living alone. That's why Gates called us in. Are you going to wait around?

MR. STIMSON. No, I think I'll come back later too. I'll walk down the hill with you, if you don't mind. This Gates— what's his connection?

MRS. BLAZER. I understand that his partner, Sam Boxby, handled Miss Culpepper's affairs—she has enough money I guess—and when he died, Gates took over. He's offered to buy her house when we find a suitable place for her to live. That's what . . . (*They exit left as she talks and* PATCH *and* SUE ELLA *enter from the right in time to see the departing figures.*)

SUE ELLA. Patch, wasn't that Mrs. Blazer who just left?

PATCH. From the Social Service—yeah. But I don't know the man.

SUE ELLA. Wonder what they wanted. (*She looks around and calls out.*) Miss Lacey, you home? (*There is a moment of silence and then the lid of the trunk is lifted and* MISS LACEY *looks out and smiles.*)

MISS LACEY. Bless you, Sue Ella, am I glad to see a friend. (*She climbs out of the trunk as she talks and comes down into the yard.*) You're the only soul I can trust.

SUE ELLA. Now Miss Lacey, that's not true. That Mrs. Blazer who just left. I'm sure you can trust her.

MISS LACEY. (*bristling*) That one least of all. (*whispers*) She wants my house.

PATCH. (*almost shouting*) Your house!

MISS LACEY. (*Notices* PATCH *for the first time and looks sharply at her. Then she speaks to* SUE ELLA.) I don't think we should talk in front of that girl.

SUE ELLA. That's Patch, Miss Lacey. She's all right. Tell me what makes you think Mrs. Blazer wants your house?

MISS LACEY. Oh, she's been coming around. I make believe I'm not here, but she pounds on the door and says Mr. Gates thinks I should move. She and that Milford Gates are in cahoots. They want my house all right.

SUE ELLA. But why?

MISS LACEY. (*looks skeptically at* PATCH *and then whispers again*) For the box, of course, the box my daddy put away for me.

PATCH. (*again almost shouting*) A treasure! You mean you've got a treasure?

SUE ELLA. Patch, you're exploding like a firecracker. (*to* MISS LACEY) A box, Miss Lacey? What kind of box?

MISS LACEY. I don't remember it exactly, but it's here some-place.

SUE ELLA. Someplace! You mean you don't know where it is?

MISS LACEY. No, I don't, but I've decided to look for it.

PATCH. I'll bet it's buried. Buried treasure! Oh boy!

MISS LACEY. Could be buried. I don't know.

SUE ELLA. What's in it?

MISS LACEY. Don't know that either.

PATCH. (*with impatience*) Well, what do you know?

SUE ELLA. Shh, Patch. (*to* MISS LACEY) If you don't know where it is, Miss Lacey, or what's in it, how do you know there is a box?

MISS LACEY. Because I've got the key. It's always been right there in that old cup on the windowsill. (*She indicates the window to the right of the door.*) And I remember the day my daddy gave it to me. "Take care of this key now, Lacey," he said. "It's important." He was already feeling poorly, and he sat there in that window seat (*She indicates the other window.*) with the blanket tucked around his knees. Then he told me about the box. "I've put it away for you," he said. "It will be safe. You just mind the key."

PATCH. It's safe all right if nobody knows where it is.

SUE ELLA. Didn't your father tell you right then what was in it?

MISS LACEY. No. He said it might as well wait until . . .

SUE ELLA. But didn't he even tell you where he put it?

MISS LACEY. That's what I can't remember. I suppose maybe he did, but like I said he was already feeling poorly and he got worse that very day and everyday after until they finally carried him away. (*Her voice drifts off in sadness and she moves away from the girls.*) Sue Ella, did you know we lost mama when I was a little girl? That was sad. But I kept my daddy until my hair turned silver. We had some fine times. (*She seems to be back in one of those fine times.*)

PATCH. Don't let her stop talking about the treasure, Sue Ella. I'm dying of curiosity.

SUE ELLA. Forget it for now, Patch. (*She turns to* MISS LACEY *and tries to lighten the mood.*) Don't be sad today, Miss Lacey. I'll help you look for the box—maybe tomorrow, but this is your birthday. We've come to wish you many happy returns—you and George. I see you have the flag out.

PATCH. Boy, I wish my birthday was on a holiday. I have to go to school. I'll bet you always had a party.

MISS LACEY. (*somberly*) I never had a party, but I remember my last birthday with mama. She baked a little cake for me and she told me I could always be right proud to have the same birthday as the first president of the United States. I closed my eyes tight, blew out the six candles and wished for George Washington to *be there.* After all, it was his birthday too. (PATCH *giggles and* SUE ELLA *pokes her to be quiet.* MISS LACEY *goes on, not even aware of the interruption.*) And he came.

PATCH. (*almost mocking*) He came? President Washington in the flesh?

MISS LACEY. Not President Washington. No—it was . . . (*She hesitates.*) If you close your eyes right now and listen to me, I'll tell you how it was.

>   (*The lights dim and after a moment of expectation*
>   MISS LACEY, *the six year old, comes out of the house.*
>   *She is dressed in the fashion of her time, and as she*
>   *runs down the steps into the yard, the twelve-year-*
>   *old* WASHINGTON *enters from the left. He is dressed*
>   *in the clothes of his day, knee breeches, buckled*
>   *shoes, and three-cornered hat. He takes off the hat*
>   *and he bows.*)

THE YOUNG MISS LACEY. You can't be George Washington. You're only a boy.

WASHINGTON. I am twelve—older than you are.

THE YOUNG MISS LACEY. But I wished for the President of the United States.

WASHINGTON. President—United States. I do not understand you.

THE YOUNG MISS LACEY. I don't believe you're Washington at all. Do you live at Mount Vernon?

WASHINGTON. I visit there, but Mount Vernon belongs to Lawrence, my half brother. It was his inheritance when my father died last year. My home is Ferry Farm with my mother. Whether or not you believe me is of no consequence.

THE YOUNG MISS LACEY. My daddy taught me to read, and I have a book about Washington. It says when he was in school he wasn't very good at grammar and his spelling was atro—atrocious. (*She stumbles over the word.*) Is it true?

WASHINGTON. I am afraid it is true. But I am good at figures, and there is no horse I cannot ride. Even my mother would attest to that.

THE YOUNG MISS LACEY. You're awful tall for twelve, but the book says you were over six-foot-two when you grew up. I guess you're Washington all right. It's just that I wanted the president.

WASHINGTON. You are a very strange girl.

PATCH. (*who can contain herself no longer, breaks into the scene being enacted before them*) You can say that again. (*At once the stage is dark, and when the lights come back on* WASHINGTON *and* THE YOUNG MISS LACEY *are gone.*)

SUE ELLA. Patch, you spoiled it. (PATCH *moves to stage left and looks off into the wings. Even though she is unbelieving, she is curious.* SUE ELLA *turns to* MISS LACEY *who had been watching entranced.*) Miss Lacey, how long did he stay?

MISS LACEY. Not very long, but it was funny that I could tell him things that would happen to him, things he didn't know about. That he would be the owner of Mount Vernon. That he would be a great general. That he would be the first president of the country. When he had to leave, he got on the horse which he'd left just beyond the edge of the yard there (*She points offstage left.*) and rode off.

SUE ELLA. Did he ever come again?

MISS LACEY. He said he would. I'm waiting.

PATCH. (*pressing the point*) You talk to him though, don't you?

MISS LACEY. Sometimes, but . . .

PATCH. There, I told you, Sue Ella. If that isn't crazy . . . (*She realizes that she is being rude and she stops, but* MISS LACEY, *offended, turns on her heels, goes to the porch, and climbs back into the trunk.*)

SUE ELLA. (*to* PATCH) Now look what you've done.

MISS LACEY. (*just before she closes the lid*) You were wrong, Sue Ella. I can't trust your friend.

SUE ELLA. You have no tact, Patch, and what's so crazy about it? When I was a little girl I had no one to play with and I invented Marietta Snow. She was with me all the time—until I started to school. If I could have Marietta, Miss Lacey could have Washington.

PATCH. But she still talks to him. She thinks he's coming back. And she's not a little girl anymore.

SUE ELLA. Maybe not, but she's lonely. You've ruined the whole day, Patch. We might as well go home.

(*As they start for the left exit,* MRS. BLAZER *enters and they almost collide with her.*)

MRS. BLAZER. (*startled*) Oh, have you seen Miss Culpepper? Has she come out at all?

SUE ELLA. I don't think she wants to talk to anybody now. (*She looks at* PATCH.)

PATCH. (*blunt as usual*) She says you want her house. Is that true?

MRS. BLAZER. Wherever did she get an idea like that? Of course I don't want her house. I am trying to find a good place for her to live where she'll be looked after. The Social Service office has been told that Miss Culpepper is incapable of taking care of herself any longer and . . .

SUE ELLA. Who's saying she can't take care of herself?

MRS. BLAZER. I don't think there's a secret about it. Mr. Gates—Milford Gates—has been the source of our information.

SUE ELLA. Gates. Hmmm. Maybe he's the one who wants the house.

MRS. BLAZER. Not "wants it" I'm sure. He did say he would buy the property to simplify things for Miss Culpepper. He says she's exceedingly forgetful and that she imagines things.

SUE ELLA. No more than a lot of people. She's smart. She's got about a million history books, and what she doesn't know about this country isn't worth knowing. Just ask her anything.

MRS. BLAZER. Frankly, I haven't had the opportunity. You see how she eludes me. I'd appreciate having a good talk with her.

PATCH. I don't think anybody ever has a good talk with her except Sue Ella. Miss Lacey pops in and out of that old trunk like a jack-in-the-box.

SUE ELLA. Patch! Why can't you button up your mouth?

MRS. BLAZER. So that's where she hides herself.

SUE ELLA. Well, I'd hide too if I thought someone wanted my house. She's all alone, Mrs. Blazer, and she hides only from people she doesn't trust.

MRS. BLAZER. (*goes to the edge of the porch and speaks to* MISS LACEY) Why don't you come out, Miss Culpepper. I know where you are, and I would really like to see you.

(MR. GATES *enters from the left in time to hear the last remark.*)

SUE ELLA. (*to* MISS LACEY) Come on, Miss Lacey, we might as well face this head-on.

(*The lid of the trunk lifts and* MISS LACEY *rises to her feet but stays in the trunk.*)

MISS LACEY. You don't need to beat around the bush, you two. (*She bobs her head toward* MRS. BLAZER *and* MR. GATES.) I know you want the box—one or the other or maybe both of you together.

MR. GATES. The box?

MRS. BLAZER. I have no idea what you're talking about, my dear. Mr. Gates has simply told me you should leave this house for your own good—find some other place to live.

MR. GATES. (*flustered*) Somewhat the other way around, Mrs. Blazer. Your people at the Social Service have told *me* Miss Culpepper shouldn't be living out here alone. I said I'd be glad to take the house off her hands when you find her a pleasant place to live.

MRS. BLAZER. There seems to be some misunderstanding. It was on your strong recommendation that the Service Center sent me out, and the reason that we are looking into a home for Miss Culpepper—"a pleasant place to live" as you say.

MISS LACEY. I have a pleasant place to live. You can't fool me. It's the box you want, and you won't get your hands on it because . . .

PATCH. Because she doesn't know where it is. That's why you can't get her treasure. She can't find it.

> (MR. STIMSON *enters from the left in time to catch the last of the conversation.*)

MR. STIMSON. Well, it looks as though I picked the right time to return.

MISS LACEY. (*without getting out of the trunk*) Just join the crowd, whoever you are.

MR. GATES. (*to* MRS. BLAZER) Who's he?

MRS. BLAZER. (*irritated with him*) I'm sure you'll find out if you listen.

MR. STIMSON. (*to* MISS LACEY) You're Miss Culpepper?

MISS LACEY. I am.

MR. STIMSON. May I introduce myself. Mr. Stimson from the County Museum. I'll come right to the point. We are interested in anything connected with George Washington, and it was suggested that you might have . . .

MISS LACEY. (*interrupting*) Another one, Sue Ella. Well, sir, I have George Washington's birthday, but you can't very well steal that from me.

MR. STIMSON. My dear Miss Culpepper, it isn't my intention to steal anything. Should you have memorabilia of Washington, we would pay you well.

MISS LACEY. You can't very well buy what's in my head, and except for the birthday that's all I have. I've read just about everything there is on Washington. My daddy saw to it that I had the books.

MR. STIMSON. Then your father was interested in Washington too?

MISS LACEY. Oh, no. Daddy bought the history books for me. His own books, and he had plenty of them, were about moneymaking and business. They're still there in that window seat where he kept them. (*She nods toward the left window.*) They don't interest me. I've never even looked at them. And I don't know that daddy ever read any of my books either.

MR. STIMSON. Well, I'm certainly your kindred spirit as far as Washington is concerned. (*He goes up onto the porch as he talks.*) Tracking down fact and fable about our first president is my particular hobby. (*He offers her his hand and assists her from the trunk.*) The man was more remarkable than the legend.

> (MISS LACEY *and* MR. STIMSON *come down off the porch to center stage, as the others listen with interest to the conversation.*)

MISS LACEY. He was only eleven when his daddy died. No chance of going off to school in England like his half brothers did.

MR. STIMSON. He managed all right. A reputation as a surveyor by the time he was fifteen and a major in the Colonial Forces before he was twenty-one. That wasn't bad.

MISS LACEY. I must say when the revolution started, the country was in good hands—good big hands.

MR. STIMSON. I've always been intrigued with the man's flaws. He had a violent temper.

MISS LACEY. (*defensively*) Which he learned to control.

> (*As* MISS LACEY *talks about* WASHINGTON *she seems to become almost a different person, positive and self-assured.*)

MR. STIMSON. You're right, and he was a good husband and stepfather. Then when he adopted Martha's grand-children, it was as though they were his own blood kin.

MISS LACEY. (*with a laugh*) The girl, Nelly he called her, had him wrapped around her finger.

MR. STIMSON. Well, to her Washington was not the great man who carved out a nation, he was just her doting father.

SUE ELLA. (*to* PATCH) OK, Patch, are you listening to all this? Crazy, huh? How much do you know about Washington?

MR. STIMSON. I'm afraid I get carried away when I talk about my favorite subject.

MRS. BLAZER. (*to* MR. GATES) Miss Culpepper seems most alert.

MISS LACEY. (*to* MR. STIMSON.) You're welcome to look through my books whenever you wish.

MR. STIMSON. I'll certainly accept that offer one of these days. But for now I won't take more of your time. (*He turns to leave.*)

PATCH. Good. Then we can get back to the treasure.

MR. STIMSON. (*With a chuckle, he turns again to the group.*) Treasure? You should be very careful using that word around a museum man. It's like lighting a fuse.

MRS. BLAZER. What do you mean, treasure?

MISS LACEY. The word is that girl's. (*She points to* PATCH *and then looks toward* MRS. BLAZER *and* MR. GATES.) And as if you two didn't know, there is a box someplace here that my daddy put away for me.

SUE ELLA. Miss Lacey, I don't think they know about it.

MR. GATES. If John Culpepper put something away, you may never find it. He didn't believe in normal protection. Said he was able to keep things safe. And as long as he knew where they were, he'd just sit back and watch the world go by.

MISS LACEY. (*suddenly jumps up in excitement*) "Sit back and watch the world go by." Milford Gates, I never liked you very much, but for once I owe you a thanks. Sue Ella, you get the cup and if I'm right, I'll get the box. (*She and* SUE ELLA *exit into the house.*)

MRS. BLAZER. (*as she watches them leave*) She doesn't act like a woman incapable of living alone.

MR. GATES. I deny saying that, you know.

MR. STIMSON. I feel like an intruder here, but I can't leave now.

MISS LACEY. (*calling out from inside the house*) Sue Ella, come here and give me a hand.

PATCH. Do you suppose she's found it? Maybe it has something to do with Washington.

MR. STIMSON. That would be too much to hope for. She said her father wasn't interested in history.

MRS. BLAZER. But he knew she was. It's possible, especially if there's any truth to the story of the ancestor at Valley Forge.

MR. GATES. I never did believe that hogwash.

PATCH. (*impatiently*) I wish they'd hurry.

(SUE ELLA *and* MISS LACEY *reenter.* SUE ELLA *has the cup and* MISS LACEY *holds aloft a small strong box.*)

MISS LACEY. It was there. In the window seat where my daddy sat to watch the world go by. Down underneath those old books of his. Sue Ella and I tossed them all out, and there it was at the bottom. Give me the key, Sue Ella. (*She and* SUE ELLA *sit on the top step of the porch with the box between them.*)

SUE ELLA. (*dumps the key from the cup and hands the key to* MISS LACEY. *Then she puts the cup down out of the way, on the steps or perhaps on the porch.*) How come you didn't look there right away, as soon as you decided you wanted to find it?

MISS LACEY. (*With shaking fingers, she tries to fit the key in the lock as she talks.*) Why would I? I knew—or thought I knew—what was in that window seat. Like I said, those books didn't interest me. There wasn't any need to disturb them. (*She pauses with a wistful look.*)

MRS. BLAZER. In all fairness, Miss Culpepper, you have been plain about not trusting at least two of us here. Would you like us to leave before you open that?

MR. STIMSON. I admit to curiosity but the lady is right, Miss Culpepper. Perhaps we should go.

MR. GATES. Well, I'm here in an official capacity. Miss Culpepper is my client.

PATCH. Please, Miss Lacey, don't make me go. I think it's too exciting.

MISS LACEY. No matter now. I told you nobody's going to get what's in here, whatever it is. I don't mind folks knowing. (*She opens the box as* SUE ELLA, PATCH, *and* MR. STIMSON *crowd around her.* MRS. BLAZER *stands politely back and* GATES *also stays in the background in spite of his declaration of his right to be there.*)

MISS LACEY. (*lifts out a small packet of papers and looks through them briefly*) Hmmm. I don't see that there's anything much here. A few pictures. Mama with me and one of mama and daddy together. And there's a letter.

PATCH. Doesn't look like much that's treasurable.

SUE ELLA. If your daddy said it was important it must be. How about the letter?

MISS LACEY. (*unfolds the single sheet of paper and reads*) "Dear Lacey, my girl, I will be gone when you read this, and though I am sorry that you are alone, you will have enough money. Sam Boxby will see that you do not want for anything." (MISS LACEY *dabs at her eyes and hands the letter to* SUE ELLA.) You read it.

(*While the letter is being read,* MR. STIMSON *picks up the cup and begins to look it over. It is not a noticeable action.*)

SUE ELLA. (*taking the letter and reading on*) "There are two things to say. First, Milford Gates wants this house —or to be more exact—this property. Someday they are going to put a development out here and he is eager to have his hands in the pot. He is not an honest man, Lacey, and will scheme in any way he can. (SUE ELLA *stops reading and looks up to see that* GATES *has eased his way toward the left exit.*) Don't let him have it. Should something happen to Boxby, turn things over to someone else. Live here until you die. It's your house. No one can take it from you.

"The other thing to say is pleasant. You come from a long proud family. I know how fascinated you have always been with Washington, since you share his birthday. There is very likely truth in the story that one of your mother's forefathers fought with the general at Valley Forge. We have no proof of this—only word of mouth. But I think you will choose to believe it.

"Live an upright life, my girl, and remember me."

(*When* SUE ELLA *finishes reading the letter there is a quiet moment, each person with his own thoughts.* MR. STIMSON, *although he has been listening, has at the same time taken a small bottle and a cloth from his pocket and has been inconspicuously rubbing the side of the cup which he still holds.*)

PATCH. (*breaks the silence*) It's so beautiful, I could cry.

MRS. BLAZER. This does put a different light on things, Mr. Gates. (*She turns to speak to him and sees him exit left.*) Well, I see he's left. Good riddance.

SUE ELLA. Then no one is going to try to make Miss Lacey leave here?

MRS. BLAZER. Certainly not I. You can stay right in your own house, Miss Culpepper, as long as you want to.

MISS LACEY. I didn't intend to do anything else.

MR. STIMSON. (*apparently intrigued with what he may have discovered*) Do you know where you got this, Miss Culpepper? (*indicates the cup*)

MISS LACEY. That old thing. Been there on the kitchen windowsill ever since I can remember.

MR. STIMSON. I could be wrong but there is a good chance that this is one of the missing Washington cups. They were made by the American silversmith, Edmund Milne, each one from sixteen silver dollars, and it looks like his signature on the bottom. There is definitely a large "W" engraved on the side. (*As he continues to rub on the cup, everyone draws around and watches with fascination.*)

MRS. BLAZER. I think I've heard about those cups. Washington's one luxury at Valley Forge during that wretched winter.

SUE ELLA. You may have a real treasure after all, Miss Lacey.

PATCH. Certainly wasn't buried.

SUE ELLA. Not even hidden away.

MISS LACEY. Daddy must not have known about it. I wonder if mama ever did?

MRS. BLAZER. I do hope it's authentic. I'm sure it would mean a great deal to you. And now, I think I'll leave too. If I can be of any help in finding a new legal adviser, let me know. Good luck again to you, Mr. Stimson. It may not have been a goose chase after all. (*She exits with good-byes all around.*)

MR. STIMSON. (*who is still holding the cup*) With your permission I'd like to take this along to have it verified. I will, of course, give you a receipt for it and a check to show good faith. You girls are witnesses to my intent.

MISS LACEY. (*thoughtfully*) I'm sorry, Mr. Stimson. I'm afraid you can't have it—at least not yet. I'd like to polish it up myself and enjoy it for awhile.

MR. STIMSON. I can understand that. But you will remember us, I hope, for the future. I'll stop by to visit again if I may. I would like to see the books.

MISS LACEY. Anytime.

(MR. STIMSON *exits and is waved off by* MISS LACEY, PATCH, *and* SUE ELLA.)

SUE ELLA. (*to* MISS LACEY) This has sure been some kind of a birthday, Miss Lacey, and everything turned out just right.

PATCH. Oh, boy, I'm sure glad I was here.

SUE ELLA. Come on, Patch, I think she wants to be alone.

MISS LACEY. You're right, Sue Ella. But come tomorrow if you like, (*She looks at* PATCH.) and I think it will be all right if you bring your friend. (SUE ELLA *and* PATCH *exit left.* MISS LACEY *stands alone at the foot of the porch steps. She picks up the cup, touching it with a kind of reverence. Then she looks off left into the wings and her face lights up.*) Glory be! (*She pauses.*) I told you you would be over six-foot-two. I am honored, Mr. President. But then I knew you would come. Don't stand out there in the shadows. Come in. I have something to show you. (*She holds out the cup; then stepping back to welcome her visitor, she makes a deep curtsy as the curtain falls.*)

PRODUCTION NOTES

Miss Lacey and the President doesn't demand a great deal in the way of a set but will be best served if you can provide what is asked for. The front of the house, with its elevated porch, its door exit, and its two prominent windows could jut out from a backdrop and shouldn't be too difficult. You could do more if you wish by adding a picket fence with a gate to enclose the yard. It would offer an opportunity for additional stage business.

The dimming of the lights is important in the Washington scene to convey a dreamlike quality, and the use of a blackout to terminate the scene will be effective. Incidentally, you might also dim the lights when Miss Lacey curtsies just before the final curtain. Even though it isn't called for in the script, it would be a good touch.

The audience should enjoy Miss Lacey's "trunk activity," and more could be made of her peeking out when no one is looking. Cues will be imperative.

The clothes the characters wear, except for those of Mr. Gates, are suggested in the script, and Mr. Gates would no doubt be dressed much like Mr. Stimson—business suit, topcoat, and hat. It is February and probably still cold. Young Washington must have an appropriate costume, but what would a Washington's Birthday play be without at least one person in colonial garb?

A few reminders. Miss Lacey says her hair turned silver before her father died. Be sure it is at least silver—could be white. Young Washington must be "tall for twelve." You wouldn't want to give the part to the shortest boy in the cast.

As for props, Mr. Stimson has a calling card, and there must be a strong box, a blackened cup, and a key. You don't have to have a tarnished silver cup, although it would be nice. Also, it isn't necessary to see the "W" that shows up with Mr. Stimson's polishing. The audience will take his word for it. There are pictures in the box and, of course, the letter. Check the script for other possibilities. Mr. Gates, for example, might carry a briefcase.

One sound effect is mentioned—the squeal of brakes. The approach of a car could be suggested simply by Miss Lacey reacting to an offstage noise—whether it is audible or not.

One final word, *Miss Lacey and the President* offers a combination of fact and fancy which can be enjoyed by actors and audience alike. Don't let a lack of proper set or lighting or costumes stop you from presenting it. Remember once you create the illusion that Miss Lacey's house is indeed there on the stage, everyone will go along with you—even to a nonexisting windowsill.

OFF GUARD

OFF GUARD

CHARACTERS

JASON STEWART, A CONTEMPORARY BOY

JILL STEWART, HIS SISTER

SCOTT, JASON'S FRIEND

AMY, JILL'S FRIEND

UNCLE HARLEY, THE GREAT-UNCLE OF JASON AND JILL

The curtain is closed when the play begins, and JASON, SCOTT, JILL, *and* AMY *enter from the left. They are on their way home from school and carry books and whatever else might be appropriate, maybe sporting equipment. It is the first of April and they are all suitably dressed for an early spring day.*

JILL. (*who is walking with* AMY *a little behind the boys, shouts to* JASON) Hey, Jason, do you know your pants are ripped?

JASON. (*without turning around*) Come on, dopey, nobody's going to fall for an April Fool joke anymore today. You might as well forget it.

JILL. Oh, you think you're so smart.

AMY. Well, he's right, Jill. If you're going to catch an April fool, it has to be first off in the morning before anybody remembers what day it is.

JASON. Even mom knows that. She got me before I was out of bed—called upstairs that I'd overslept and if I wasn't out the door in ten minutes I'd miss the bus. Wow! I never moved so fast. If I'm late to school once more I'm in trouble.

SCOTT. So? What time was it?

JILL. (*laughs*) Six-thirty. We don't even have to get up until eight.

JASON. You don't need to laugh. I got you at breakfast. Ask her how she likes her hot chocolate with dad's shaving foam instead of whipped cream.

JILL. I had my mind on more important things. Mom said Uncle Harley was coming today from Alaska. I was thinking about him.

AMY. I don't ever catch anybody. I always giggle and give it away.

JASON. Hey, I forgot about Uncle Harley. We better hurry. Anyhow, you can knock off the April fooling until next year.

JILL. Not necessarily, Mr. Know-it-all.

SCOTT. Well, you'd sure have to find somebody who doesn't know anything about April Fool's Day.

AMY. That wouldn't be easy around here.

JILL. You just have to catch somebody off guard, that's all.

JASON. Well, I bet you can't. And I'll give you the rest of the day. If you fool anybody before bedtime, I'll do your house chores for the next two weeks.

JILL. Hmmm. OK. It's a deal.

JASON. But if you lose I get the same services. Remember that means cleaning out my hamster cage. Come on, Scott, I want to see if Uncle Harley's there. (*They exit right, leaving* AMY *and* JILL *still on stage.*)

JILL. (*calling after* JASON) Don't be too sure of yourself, Jason Stewart.

AMY. I don't think that was a good bet, Jill. Who do you think you can fool?

JILL. I wish it could be that brother of mine.

AMY. No way.

JILL. Yeah. He'd be suspicious of anything now. But I was thinking maybe Uncle Harley. Mom had a meeting this afternoon. She said if he was there when we came home to look after him until she got back. (*They exit right, as* JILL *continues to talk.*) I've got a couple of . . .

(*The curtain opens on the living room of the Stewart home. Upstage on the right wall there is a window which looks onto the street. The outside door is downstage on the same wall, and at center back, French doors open to a patio or garden, a bit of which might be visible. The exit at left stage leads to the rest of the house. The furnishings are contemporary—a davenport perhaps, an occasional table, a couple of chairs, lamps, and whatever else lends itself to modest but comfortable living. Two suitcases stand by the left exit, and a heavy plaid jacket is draped over one of the chairs. JASON and SCOTT enter from the right.)*

JASON. (*looking about and spotting the jacket and the luggage*) He came all right. There are his things.

SCOTT. You never said you had an uncle in Alaska.

JASON. He's really mom's uncle. He has a lumber camp up near Fairbanks.

SCOTT. That's neat.

JASON. That's not the best. He comes down to see us about once a year, and he stops off someplace on the way to buy presents. Then he gives us money, and I mean *money*—checks. Come on, let's see if he's on the patio. You'll like him. (*They exit through the French doors as* JILL *and* AMY *enter from the right.*)

AMY. Uncle Harley sounds like Santa Claus. I wish I had an uncle like that. My relatives keep their money to themselves.

JILL. I guess it's because we're his only family. He never married. I wonder where he is.

(*The boys return from the patio.* UNCLE HARLEY *was not there.*)

JASON. He's here someplace—maybe upstairs.

AMY. Jill's going to pull an April Fool on him, Jason. It just might work.

JASON. You aren't going to catch Uncle Harley. He's been around.

JILL. Up there in the wilds, yes. He won't be expecting it.

JASON. I don't think you should do it, Jill. If we're supposed to be nice to him . . .

JILL. (*interrupting*) Aren't you the considerate one all of a sudden? It wouldn't be because you might lose the bet?

JASON. Of course not.

JILL. Anyhow I'm not going to hurt him. And you better not spoil it. Amy's my witness. Now listen. Uncle Harley's going to have a phone call from Mr. Fox, and when he answers . . .

JASON AND SCOTT IN UNISON. Mr. Fox will say he would like to have him come down to the zoo to meet him.

He's in cage fifty-two. (*They laugh.*) No one will fall for that old gag.

JILL. Why not? Uncle Harley's been in Alaska a long time.

AMY. (*who has wandered over to the window on the right wall*) There's an old man coming up the walk.

JILL. Good. We'll do it right away and get it over with. Amy, you're Mr. Fox's secretary. Go in the den and use dad's business phone. I'll answer. Give us a few minutes. Count to three hundred or something. And remember he's Mr. Miller, Mr. Harley Miller. (AMY *exits to the left and almost at once the front door opens to admit* UNCLE HARLEY. *He is an old man, but robust, obviously from his outdoor life.*)

UNCLE HARLEY. (*in a brusque, hearty voice*) Well, now, here are my young people. (*He goes to* SCOTT, *apparently mistaking him for* JASON.) Jason, my boy, how are you?

JASON. No, Uncle Harley, I'm Jason. That's my friend Scott.

SCOTT. Glad to meet you, sir. Jason's been telling me about you.

UNCLE HARLEY. All bad I'm sure. And Jason, I should have looked at you closer. You've got your mother's eyes. (*He turns to* JILL.) But you're Jill. No mistake there.

You both grow though. Every time I come you've shot up a little farther.

JILL. Mom said you might be here when we got home. What time did you get here?

UNCLE HARLEY. It was after lunch, but before your mother left. She said I could go on upstairs and unpack but I wasn't in any hurry. Been out for a walk as a matter of fact.

JASON. How's the lumber camp?

UNCLE HARLEY. Fine. Fine as frog's hair. At least when I left it.

> (*The phone rings and* JILL *answers it while* JASON *and* SCOTT *and* UNCLE HARLEY *go on talking in low tones.*)

JILL. (*turning from the phone with feigned surprise*) It's for you, Uncle Harley. Did you expect a call?

UNCLE HARLEY. For me? Is it long distance?

JILL. With direct dialing you never know. The girl said a Mr. Fox—yes, Fox, that was it—wanted to talk to Mr. Harley Miller. That's you.

UNCLE HARLEY. It is, unless somebody's changed my name without telling me. Must be long distance. I don't know

who'd be calling though. Fox . . . Hmmm. I'll bet it's
that new foreman they were going to put on at the mill.
(*He has moved to the phone and now speaks into the
mouthpiece.*) Look here now, Fox, or whatever your
name is, I'm on a holiday and don't want to be disturbed. Any problem you have can wait until I get
back. (*He hangs up without waiting for a response from
the other end of the line. Then he turns to* JILL.) I
ought to know better than to tell anybody where I'm
going. Well, I guess I'll take my things up to my room.
Be right back. Your mother said the room at the top of
the stairs. Right? (*He moves to the left exit and picks
up the suitcases as he speaks.*)

JILL. Right, Uncle Harley. That's the guest room. Let me
know if you need anything.

(UNCLE HARLEY *exits and when he is gone* JILL,
SCOTT, *and* JASON *exchange looks of question.*)

JASON. Well, it didn't work.

SCOTT. Maybe he knew the joke after all.

JILL. I don't think so. He had such a straight face—never
batted an eye. You didn't wink at him, did you, Jason?

JASON. Of course I didn't. You were right here watching
me. Anyhow, you didn't fool him.

JILL. I haven't given up yet.

(AMY *enters from the left.*)

AMY. He didn't give me a chance.

JILL. I know. But I've got another idea, a better one. Let me tell you fast before he comes back. There's a piece of that chocolate cake left. Mom never did get around to icing it and I'll put a real thick gooey frosting on it and . . .

SCOTT. What's tricky about that? Your mom's cakes are great with or without frosting.

JILL. Have you ever tasted my hot pepper sauce frosting?

SCOTT. No thanks.

JILL. And Jason, don't you even look sideways. Amy, you watch him if Uncle Harley comes back before I do. It won't take me long. I know there's a can of frosting on the shelf. (*She exits left.*)

JASON. (*pretending to be offended*) My sister doesn't trust me.

(UNCLE HARLEY reenters from the left.)

UNCLE HARLEY. I didn't bother to unpack—can do that later. And who is this young lady?

AMY. I'm Amy, a friend of Jill's. She says you're from Alaska. We've been studying Alaska in school. You can give me some inside information.

UNCLE HARLEY. I'll do that, Amy. Any time.

SCOTT. Jason told me about your lumber camp. Sounds great.

UNCLE HARLEY. Lonely sometimes. After all, I started out as a city boy. Grew up right around here. But I like being a woodsman.

SCOTT. I think I'd like it too. Maybe I'll be a ranger when I get out of school.

UNCLE HARLEY. That's the boy. (*He slaps* SCOTT *on the back and then wanders upstage to look out into the patio as he talks.*) It's a good life. No fences. No highways to speak of. No supermarkets. Not too many people and just rough country. Isn't much of that left anymore.

AMY. (*aside to the boys*) Jill just might win on this one.

(JILL *enters from the left with the cake, a large square of it. She puts the plate, along with a fork and a napkin, on the occasional table.*)

JILL. Mom said we should make you feel at home, Uncle Harley, and I thought maybe you'd like to have a little refreshment. It's mom's special chocolate cake. You can sit right here if you want to. (*She pulls a straight chair over to the occasional table for him.*)

UNCLE HARLEY. Well, that's mighty nice of you, girl, but you know I'll just have to pass on cake. Doctor says no sweets. That's one of those plagues of getting old. I'll tell you what. I'll just divvy this up for the four of you, and I'll have what I'm allowed. Always carry a few sunflower seeds in my pocket. Wouldn't be polite to let you eat alone. (*Using the fork, he divides the cake as he talks.*)

SCOTT. (*wanting to get out of it*) None for me, thanks. I'd better get on home. See you later, Jason. (*He starts to leave.*)

UNCLE HARLEY. (*puts a hand out to detain him*) You can't go without a piece of cake. There's a bit for all of you. Just sit yourself down there. (*He virtually pushes him into the chair beside the occasional table and hands him a portion of the cake on the napkin.*) Be glad your innards don't talk back to you. (*Then he hands the others their portions.*) You don't need forks. Fingers were made before forks anyhow.

AMY. (*tries to refuse*) My mother says I shouldn't eat sweets either, Uncle Harley. Between meals at least.

JASON. Yeah, even when you're a kid you can't always eat what you want. There are always rules.

UNCLE HARLEY. Come on now. Just this once. Special occasion when old Harley visits. A lot of little rules fly out the window. Isn't that right, Jill?

JILL. I guess so, Uncle Harley.

(*There is nothing for them to do but accept the cake and eat it. When they encounter the hot pepper,* AMY *coughs and the others squirm and grimace.* HARLEY *munches away on his seeds.*)

UNCLE HARLEY. That sure looks good, kids. I know your mother's baking.

JASON. (*with effort*) It's good all right.

SCOTT. Yeah, good. (*He tries to keep from eating the frosting by pushing some of it off onto the napkin.*) Delicious. (AMY *doesn't say anything. She continues to cough and sputter, and as soon as she has gulped down the cake she moves toward the front door.*)

AMY. I do have to go now, (*She coughs again.*) and I'd better hurry.

SCOTT. Me too, Uncle Harley. Bye. (AMY *and* SCOTT *exit.*)

UNCLE HARLEY. I like your friends. Nice kids. Well, now I think it's about check time. This year I didn't bring any presents. To tell the truth you're too old for toys and I didn't know what to buy. Excuse me a minute. I'm sure there's a pen in your dad's study. I'll be right back.

(*He exits left and while he is gone* JASON *and* JILL, *reacting to the peppery icing, fan their mouths.*)

JILL. How did I know he couldn't eat cake?

JASON. Do you think he knows what you're up to? I'm beginning to wonder.

JILL. Not unless you told him. Besides, what would be the point if he doesn't let us know he knows. He didn't say "April Fool."

JASON. Anyhow I think you might as well give up for sure now.

(UNCLE HARLEY *reenters from the left.*)

UNCLE HARLEY. Like I said, I don't know what to buy you anymore, so you'll find the checks are a little bigger this year. (*He sits at the table, writes out the checks, and hands them to* JILL *and* JASON.) You won't mind doing your own shopping I hope.

JILL. (*as she looks at the check*) Mind! Of course not. But Uncle Harley, this is too much.

JASON. (*looks at his check too*) A hundred dollars! Wow!

UNCLE HARLEY. Well, I'm not sure when, or even if, I'll get back again. I'm getting to be an old codger you know.

JILL. I don't think mom will want us to take this much.

UNCLE HARLEY. It's all right. I checked with her before she left.

(JASON *and* JILL *both pocket the checks.*)

JASON. I've been trying to save for a new bike. This will about do it.

JILL. And I want a T.V. set all my own. I've almost got enough with this.

(*They run to* UNCLE HARLEY *and* JILL *hugs him while* JASON *pumps his arm in thanks.*)

UNCLE HARLEY. Don't make me cry, kids. It's my pleasure. (*He suddenly listens to something offstage right.*) I think I hear your mother's car. She was going to market before she came home. Maybe she can use some help. (*He exits right.*)

JILL. You know I'm glad my tricks didn't work. Maybe I would have hurt his feelings. I don't care if I do lose the bet.

JASON. (*has taken the check out of his pocket and is looking at it*) Jill, my check's blank. Look at yours.

JILL. (*looks at hers*) Mine is too. Disappearing ink!

(*As the joke dawns on them,* UNCLE HARLEY *pokes his head in the door right.*)

UNCLE HARLEY. April Fool, kids. Your Uncle Harley was on to you. He may have come out of the woods but not down out of the trees.
(*quick curtain*)

(*After a brief moment, the curtain goes up again for the epilogue.* JILL *is alone in the living room as* JASON *enters from the left.*)

JILL. Well, somebody got fooled.

JASON. But you didn't do the fooling. I'll give you a list of my chores first thing in the morning. And be gentle with my hamster.

JILL. Don't rub it in. Anyhow Uncle Harley said he'd give us new checks, and I sure love the earrings he brought me. (*She pushes her hair back to display her earrings.*)

JASON. I thought he didn't bring presents.

JILL. That was just a part of his April Fool joke. If you hadn't hurried off to brag to Scott about winning the bet, you'd have gotten yours. He left it there for you. (*She indicates the package beside the davenport.*)

JASON. (*picks up the box and sets it on the table*) Oh boy, I wonder what it is. (*He tears off the wrapping.*) That soccer ball I wanted, I bet. (*He opens the box and pulls out all the paper and finally a black plastic bag. He tears it open impatiently.*) What's this? Whew! Garbage?

JILL. April Fool, smarty. One of my chores is to take out the garbage, and you might as well start tonight.

(*quick curtain*)

PRODUCTION NOTES

The first day of April! And please, in a busy world enjoy the luxury of a day set aside for pranks and harmless mischief. *Off Guard* is meant to be presented in the spirit of such levity.

There is certainly no problem in production, no matter how limited your facilities. If you have someone introduce the play who will describe the living room of the Stewart home, you don't have to worry about actual doors and windows. Before one exit, the boys say they are going to look for Uncle Harley in the patio. No question that they are going through those French doors. And when Amy says she sees an old man coming up the walk, the audience will know she is at the window.

The opening scene in front of the curtain is short, but its tempo should be maintained as the characters move across the stage. Give them some kind of activity. Maybe the boys could be bouncing volleyballs or tossing a baseball back and forth. Again, the stage business can be molded to fit your community and school. You will have ideas.

This is a contemporary play and should be kept up to date. Change the dialogue and dress according to the mode of your area. Just one thing, Jill and Jason must have pockets for Uncle Harley's checks.

Develop the character of Uncle Harley. He is old-fashioned and backwoodsy, but he is nobody's fool. You will have to make him believable if you want his April Fool joke to come off.

Develop the business of eating the cake, too. There is

an opportunity for a great deal of byplay while Jill, Amy, Jason, and Scott eat the hot pepper frosting under Uncle Harley's watchful eyes.

As for props, you will need whatever the characters are carrying home from school in the first scene. You will need a telephone, Uncle Harley's suitcases and jacket, his checkbook, and the pen he gets from the den. Jill can wear the earrings throughout the play as long as they cannot be seen.

Don't forget to put the wrapped package at the end of the davenport before the last scene. But waste no time getting to the garbage bag and the punch line.

If interest in April Fool's Day has faded in your community, now is the time to brighten it up. Putting on a play might help.

LUDLILLIAN AND THE DARK ROAD

LUDLILLIAN AND THE DARK ROAD

CHARACTERS

LUDLILLIAN, THE WAYWARD WITCH

LILLY, HER CONSCIENCE

TROLL, THE LEADER OF THE BENEVOLENT SOCIETY OF
   SPOOKS AND SPELLCASTERS

THE LITTLE GHOST, THE NEWEST MEMBER OF THE SOCIETY

THE ENVOY FROM THE MALEVOLENT LEAGUE

THE GIRL WITH THE BEAUTEOUS HAT

ELSIE, THE GIRL WHO BELONGS OUT THERE

OTHER MEMBERS OF THE BENEVOLENT SOCIETY, AS MANY
   AS DESIRED

OTHER CHILDREN FROM OUT THERE, AS MANY AS DESIRED

THE TIME: *All Hallow E'en*

The opening scene takes place in front of the closed curtain. Ghosts, goblins, and other creatures of a fantasy world enter from the right. As they hurry across the stage toward the left exit, there is a general buzzing of conversation. "What time is it?" "We don't want to miss the meeting." "We're not late." "Come on."

They are no sooner offstage than another group enters from the right. LILLY *is among them. She is dressed like a witch except that she is entirely in white from her tall, peaked hat right down to her shoes, including the shopping bag which she clutches in one hand. As this second group reaches center stage,* THE ENVOY *from The Malevolent League strides in, also from the right. He is a dark figure in a great brown cape with a hood which conceals his face. The crowd draws back in fear to let him pass. Again there is the buzzing of conversation, this time in hushed tones. "Give him room." "It's* THE ENVOY *from across the river." "Stay out of his way."* THE ENVOY *moves across the stage and exits left. After he is gone, everyone is motionless for a moment watching the exit as though afraid he might return. Then all exit left.*

LUDLILLIAN *enters from the right. She would be a duplicate of* LILLY *even to the shopping bag except for the fact that she is in black, and instead of the standard witch's hat she wears bright flowers in her hair. She moves in a dawdling fashion. Does a little dance step and stops to curtsy to the audience. The* LITTLE GHOST *enters from the right and when he passes* LUDLILLIAN *she catches hold of the white mantle which envelops him.*

LUDLILLIAN. Hey kid, what's your hurry?

LITTLE GHOST. Please let go of me. I've got to get to the meeting. I don't want to be late.

LUDLILLIAN. It doesn't matter as long as you get there in time to pick up your assignment. That's all that's necessary.

LITTLE GHOST. Assignment? I don't understand. This is my first Halloween. (*He tries to break away.*) Oh, please, please let me go.

(LUDLILLIAN *pulls him around by his mantle, teasing him. She lets go of him with one hand and then catches him with the other while he continues to protest.* LILLY *enters from the left.*)

LILLY. (*to* LUDLILLIAN) How did we get separated?

LUDLILLIAN. (*still teasing the* LITTLE GHOST) It wasn't easy. You always stick so close.

LILLY. Close! I should be more than close. You know we're supposed to be in the same skin.

LUDLILLIAN. Shh. You don't have to tell everybody that you're my conscience. My lily-white Lilly. Yuk. Just once I wish I could be free of you.

LILLY. Don't wish that. You'd be in a fine witch's stew if I wasn't around. As soon as you get out of my sight you're into mischief. And why are you teasing the little fellow?

LUDLILLIAN. I'm not hurting him. (LILLY *tries to come close to* LUDLILLIAN *who runs away, pulling the* LITTLE GHOST *with her.*) You just keep your distance, Lilly.

LITTLE GHOST. (*to* LILLY) Please ask her to let me go. I have to get to the meeting.

LUDLILLIAN. I'm trying to tell him the meeting's not important and Troll's a bore. Who wants to hear that long story about the great conflict and the treaty?

LILLY. There are new spirits who haven't heard it.

LITTLE GHOST. I haven't.

LILLY. You see.

LUDLILLIAN. I still say it's a waste of time. All anybody needs to know is that on Halloween the children *Out There* aren't afraid of us. They dress up and pretend to be witches and goblins and ghosts and whatever. We can go trick-or-treating with them, play games, have fun. *We* can pretend to be children.

LILLY. But there are rules. Now let go of him. (*She has managed to get close enough to put her hands over LUD-LILLIAN's and the LITTLE GHOST is released.*) Run along, little fellow. You may already be late. (*The LITTLE GHOST runs offstage left and LILLY turns to LUDLILLIAN.*) And another thing, where's your hat? You know a proper witch has to wear her hat on all important occasions.

LUDLILLIAN. It's in my bag. (*She pats the shopping bag in annoyance.*) I'll put it on when I get to the assembly hall.

LILLY. I doubt that you'd get there without me. You know it wouldn't hurt to hear Troll discuss the rules again.

LUDLILLIAN. I know the rules. (*mimics* TROLL) Commit no transgression, and get back to the gate by midnight. (*resumes her own voice*) You know I always get through the gates before the last stroke of twelve. And have I ever done anything wrong? I mean really wrong? Don't worry.

LILLY. Well, I do worry. If The Envoy ever succeeds in tricking you, I won't be able to help. Come on. (*She pulls* LUDLILLIAN *off left as the curtain opens on the assembly hall. There are a number of large empty packing boxes lying about, and upstage center there is a great gate which is closed and secured with an enormous padlock. Above the gate there is a sign—The Benevolent Society of Spooks and Spellcasters.*

Witches, elves, and other fantasy creatures, including those who passed across the stage earlier, are listening with rapt attention to TROLL, *who is at right center presiding from behind one of the boxes. On it rests a great ledger and a pile of papers.*)

TROLL. (*speaking in the voice* LUDLILLIAN *had imitated*) Now that you have heard once more the history of *The Benevolent Society*, we are ready to begin the Halloween caper. We have gone over all the regulations as set down in the ancient treaty, but I repeat: commit no transgression, and get back to the gate by midnight. You are dismissed.

(*One of the elves starts to remove the padlock when there is a banging on the gate and the voice of* THE ENVOY *is heard.*)

THE ENVOY. I am The Envoy of Wocan. Let me in! I am expected.

(*The elf hesitates, but* TROLL *waves him on and when the gate swings open* THE ENVOY *strides into the hall.*)

TROLL. You may be expected but you are not welcome.

THE ENVOY. You know why I come. If any one of you com-
mits the slightest transgression or stays one moment past
the allotted time, he truly belongs to the masters of
transgression—*The Malevolent League.* I am delegated
to take the offender across the river.

TROLL. We've never lost anybody yet. Why don't you
give up?

THE ENVOY. Never. (*He looks around the hall.*) There is
one of you who is marked. I shall stand by. (*He exits
through the gateway as the* LITTLE GHOST *runs in from
the left.*)

TROLL. (*to the* LITTLE GHOST) You are late.

LITTLE GHOST. I'm sorry about that, your leadership. I—I
was held back.

TROLL. (*who has been looking in the ledger*) You're the
new one, aren't you? A very bad beginning. What's your
name?

LITTLE GHOST. I don't think I have a name, your leadership.
Nobody told me.

TROLL. No matter. Ghosts are better off without names. Sit
over there until I can figure out what to do with you.
(*He indicates a small box off to the right and then*

speaks to the general assembly.) All right, everybody, on your way. Enjoy the night, but remember the conditions.

(*The crowd begins to drift offstage through the gateway, ignoring the* LITTLE GHOST *who sits on his box with a sad look on his face.* LILLY *and* LUD-LILLIAN, *who now wears her black hat, enter from the left.* LILLY *is behind* LUDLILLIAN, *pushing her. The* LITTLE GHOST *perks up when he sees them and he listens to their conversation.*)

LUDLILLIAN. All right, we're here. You can stop pushing. (*She approaches* TROLL.) Where's my assignment?

TROLL. (*fumbles around among his papers for an envelope which he hands to* LUDLILLIAN *as he speaks*) Ludlillian, you are a disgrace to *The Society.*

LUDLILLIAN. I pay my dues.

TROLL. That's about all. I can't understand how you got into our ranks in the first place. Someone must have tampered with the records. I think you really belong across the river.

LILLY. I try my best to stay with her, Troll.

LUDLILLIAN. You know I don't do any evil. It's just that nobody wants me to have any fun, and I could enjoy myself a good deal more if I didn't have her on my back. (*She indicates* LILLY.)

TROLL. Of course she shouldn't be on your back. She should be in your head. Everybody else's conscience is a part of him. You're the only member of *The Society* who can't keep herself together. Mind your step tonight. I think The Envoy has his eye on you.

LUDLILLIAN. He doesn't frighten me in the least. I've always been in the clear. (*She sees the* LITTLE GHOST.) What's the matter with the kid?

TROLL. I almost forgot. He's the new one, and he came in late. I'm not sure what to do with him.

LILLY. (*to* LUDLILLIAN) His being late was your fault, you know.

TROLL. (*to* LUDLILLIAN) Then I guess you're the one to take care of him. Be sure to tell him about The Envoy and *The Malevolent League.*

(TROLL *motions for the* LITTLE GHOST *to come over to him and he does so.*)

LUDLILLIAN. Oh, for heaven's sake, it's bad enough to be stuck with Lilly. Do I have to have him too?

TROLL. Wait a minute. (*to* LILLY) Lilly, I'll put you in charge. That way he'll get through the night. At least he'll have a ghost of a chance.

LUDLILLIAN. Very funny.

TROLL. Now that that is settled I can get on to my own assignment. I'm off to Center City. They're hiding a cow in the library. (TROLL *exits through the gateway.*)

LILLY. (*to the* LITTLE GHOST) Now where shall we begin?

LITTLE GHOST. I have a lot of questions. What's The Malevol—that league? And who's The Envoy? And why does she (*indicates* LUDLILLIAN) belong across the river? And what does benevolent mean? I am a brand-new ghost. I don't know anything.

LUDLILLIAN. You can say that twice.

LITTLE GHOST. All of it or just that I don't know anything?

LUDLILLIAN. (*with a gesture of disbelief*) There is no hope for him.

LILLY. (*Puts her arm around the* LITTLE GHOST *and leads him over to one of the boxes at left center. He climbs up on the box and* LILLY *sits beside him and begins to tell the tale.*) I might as well begin at the beginning. (LUDLILLIAN *shakes her head in impatience and paces the floor as* LILLY *talks.*) A long, long, long time ago the world of fancy—our world—was united. Everyone walked hand in hand in peace and light.

LUDLILLIAN. (*groans*) I can see this is going to take a long, long, long time.

LILLY. (*giving* LUDLILLIAN *a look of irritation*) No one ever ventured down the dark road. No one even thought about the murky river. Everyone in *The Benevolent Society* was content and on Halloween we went *Out There* to meet the children with no time limit. (*She sighs.*) Then something happened.

LUDLILLIAN. (*stops pacing long enough to interrupt again*) Wocan got curious. That's what happened.

LILLY. That's right. One day he wandered down the dark road. He crossed the murky river. He discovered—Evil. Then he decided there was more power in evil than in good, and he gathered his wicked friends around him and started *The Malevolent League.*

LUDLILLIAN. Get to the point.

LILLY. (*ignores her*) There is always struggle between good and evil and naturally there was a great conflict.

LITTLE GHOST. What happened?

LILLY. Well, both sides suffered, but it ended in a draw.

LUDLILLIAN. You're as bad as Troll.

LITTLE GHOST. (*to* LILLY) Go on.

LILLY. Well, they signed a treaty. First of all, because we didn't want to mingle with Wocan and his kind, Halloween was divided into two shifts. We have until midnight; they have from midnight until dawn. And also we agreed that if Wocan would leave us alone through the rest of the year, we would abide by his rules for this one night. We are fair game until twelve o'clock. The Envoy has a right to do what he can to catch any one of us. We must be very careful or we might end up across the river.

LUDLILLIAN. You've talked long enough, Lilly. (*to the* LITTLE GHOST) That's about all there is to it, kid. We're the good guys and over there—they're the bad guys. Halloween is still the greatest night of the year. Come on.

LILLY. I won't budge until you change your attitude. The little fellow doesn't know anything about the transgressions.

LUDLILLIAN. (*shrugs*) OK. You tell him. Take all the time you want. It's all right with me. I'll go on alone. (*As she starts to leave,* LILLY *grabs her.*)

LILLY. No you won't. I still have something to say about what you do. (*She pulls* LUDLILLIAN *over to one of the boxes and sets her down on it.*) You just sit there and be patient.

> (LUDLILLIAN *gets to her feet and pushes* LILLY *away.* LILLY *shakes her.* LUDLILLIAN *stamps on* LILLY'*s foot. They have a hair-pulling fight.* LILLY *ends up on the floor, dazed and helpless.* LUDLILLIAN *drags one of*

*the empty boxes over from the right side of the hall
and puts it over* LILLY. *Then she hoists another box
on top of the first.* LILLY *is trapped.*)

LUDLILLIAN. (*turning to the* LITTLE GHOST) Now if you
want to see Halloween, come with me.

LILLY. (*pounds on the box which entraps her*) Let me out
—let me out.

LITTLE GHOST. I don't think you should have done that.

LUDLILLIAN. She's my conscience and if my conscience
doesn't bother me she shouldn't bother you. (*She exits
through the gateway pulling the* LITTLE GHOST *along
with her as* LILLY *continues to shout.*)

(*The curtain closes and in a moment* THE ENVOY
*enters from the right. He pushes the hood from his
head and we see his face—that of a devil. Quickly
he puts on the mask of a smiling monk and adjusts
the hood like a cowl so that his masked face is in
full view. He ties a rope around his waist and
around his neck he puts a chain with a cross at the
end. He does not speak and keeps in the background when* LUDLILLIAN *enters left with the* LITTLE
GHOST *hanging on to her skirt. Neither of them no-
tice* THE ENVOY *because they are absorbed in their
own conversation.*)

LITTLE GHOST. I still don't know what I'm supposed to do.

LUDLILLIAN. Do! You're supposed to have fun. I intend to, and you might as well face it, kid, you'll have to take care of yourself. (*She starts to leave.*)

LITTLE GHOST. I wish you wouldn't leave me. I'm afraid.

LUDLILLIAN. Afraid of what? The children? They're only pretending to be witches and goblins and ghosts. You're the real thing. If the children knew that, they'd be the ones afraid. If you could look deep into your own eyes, you'd understand.

LITTLE GHOST. But Lilly said something about trans—(*He has difficulty with the word.*) transgressions. I don't even know what that means. And she said we have to be careful. Of what?

LUDLILLIAN. Just be careful you don't step in a puddle of black paint. What a nuisance you are. Like I said, have fun and get back to the gate by midnight. And you know you can bring a souvenir for yourself too if you want—something that takes your fancy. But look, kid, I could stand here all night explaining about the trans-gressions. (*She digs into her shopping bag and produces a sheaf of papers which she hands to him.*) Here's a copy of the treaty. It will tell you everything you should know. Read it for yourself.

LITTLE GHOST. But Ludlillian, there's something *you* should know. I . . .

(LUDLILLIAN *doesn't wait. She is out the left exit.*
THE ENVOY *also exits right without having been
seen. The* LITTLE GHOST *looks at the papers and then
puts them in an inner pocket and exits left.*)

(*The curtain opens on a street scene. There are
costumed children milling around talking and
laughing. One is dressed as a rabbit, one girl is a
Southern belle of the Civil War days, looking awk-
ward and uncomfortable in a hoop skirt and flowered garden hat. Another girl,* ELSIE, *is a ghost, and
her costume, all white, is in two pieces. The head
covering, with holes for eyes and mouth, is topped
with a bright red bow.*

LUDLILLIAN *enters left with* THE ENVOY *not far
behind her although she is not aware of him. She
pops one child's balloon, upsets another's trick-or-
treat sack, dances around the stage. She sees the
Southern belle and walks over to her.*)

LUDLILLIAN. What a beautiful dress you have.

THE GIRL. (*pops her bubble gum and digs into her bag for
another piece*) I think it's dumb, but I had to wear it.
My mother spent weeks sewing on the thing. It has
three petticoats. I'm supposed to be Scarlett O'Hara. Do
I look like Scarlett?

LUDLILLIAN. I wouldn't know about that. But you have a
beauteous hat.

THE GIRL. It's silly—all these ribbons and flowers. I really wanted to be a witch. I like your hat better. I'll trade.

LUDLILLIAN. Hmmm. (*She sighs.*) Sorry, I can't do that.

THE GIRL. Why not?

LUDLILLIAN. You wouldn't understand.

THE GIRL. But you didn't answer the question. Why not?

>(THE ENVOY, *who has been watching, has sidled up to* LUDLILLIAN *and now speaks to her.*)

THE ENVOY. Yes. Why not?

LUDLILLIAN. (*does not recognize him because of his disguise*) Friar Tuck, I presume. Well, I don't expect you to understand either, but I have to wear this hat to—well on certain occasions. Lilly says so.

THE GIRL. Lilly?

THE ENVOY. (*looking around innocently*) No one seems to be watching you.

LUDLILLIAN. That's true. And I'm getting along very well without her.

THE GIRL. (*impatiently*) Do you want to trade or not?

LUDLILLIAN. Hmmm. (*She looks around as though she expects* LILLY *to appear.*) It's a deal. (*They trade hats and* LUDLILLIAN *struts about pleased with herself.*)

THE ENVOY. (*rubbing his hands in glee*) Most becoming. (*aside*) Ludlillian without her conscience is putty in my hands. (*Back to* LUDLILLIAN) You know it's a shame you aren't a real witch. You could have more fun. You could turn that little rabbit over there into a toad. (*He indicates the child in the rabbit costume.*)

LUDLILLIAN. Who says I'm not . . . (*She catches herself.*) Well, magical things happen on Halloween. I could try. A toad would be nice. (LUDLILLIAN, *excited about the prospect, dances across the stage toward the rabbit. She takes a wand from her shopping bag and starts to wave it over the rabbit when there is a faint sound from offstage.*)

THE VOICE OF LILLY. Let me out. Let me out. (*There is muffled pounding.*)

LUDLILLIAN. (*hesitates*) I don't know. I'm afraid Lilly wouldn't like it.

THE ENVOY. (*who has followed her over to the rabbit*) What difference does that make? This Lilly of yours can't stop you if she isn't here. Come on, Ludlillian, do the toad.

LUDLILLIAN. (*looks at him critically*) What did you say? You called me Ludlillian. I didn't tell you my name.

THE ENVOY. (*realizing his mistake*) Oh, you must have. Hurry, do the toad and let's go find some excitement.

LUDLILLIAN. (*who has been studying him*) I see who you are now. Of course you know my name. You're The Envoy from across the river. (*She snatches off his monk mask to reveal the devil face.*)

THE ENVOY. (*quickly pulling the cowl up over his head*) All right, I admit it. But you do want to do the toad, don't you?

LUDLILLIAN. Forget the toad. You just want me to do something evil. You also want to keep me busy so that I'll be late. But I always get back on time.

THE ENVOY. That's when you have Lilly with you. She's the one who sees to it that you reach the gate by midnight. But you left Lilly behind.

LUDLILLIAN. You don't need a conscience to make you want to save your skin.

THE ENVOY. Come now, don't you really want to go down the dark road and across the river with me?

(*There is a faint pounding noise offstage.*)

THE VOICE OF LILLY. (*barely audible*) Let me out. Let me out.

THE ENVOY. You're basically bad, Ludlillian, basically bad.

LUDLILLIAN. I am not. Absolutely, definitely, positively not. (THE ENVOY *grabs her arm, but she pulls away and runs downstage left.*)

THE VOICE OF LILLY. (*getting weaker*) Let me out.

LUDLILLIAN. (*speaking out into the theater*) Lilly! I'm sorry. I'm truly sorry. I do need you. I do. (*She runs back to the girl, exchanges the flowered hat for her own, and exits left as the curtain closes.*)

(*The* LITTLE GHOST *enters from the right in front of the closed curtain. He is crying.* ELSIE, *in her ghost costume, enters from the left.*)

ELSIE. Are you crying because you didn't get any candy? You can have some of mine.

LITTLE GHOST. That's not the trouble. Ludlillian left me.

ELSIE. Ludlillian? That's a funny name. Is she your sister?

LITTLE GHOST. No, just a witch. She said I should take care of myself and have a good time.

ELSIE. And you're not, are you?

LITTLE GHOST. I wouldn't be crying if I was having any fun.

ELSIE. I'm not having any fun either. My sister left me. She wanted to go around with her friends. I don't like trick-or-treating alone. It's funny we're both ghosts. But it sure gets stuffy under this hood. (*She takes off the hood section of her costume and stuffs it in her sack.*) I don't really care whether I have a costume anyhow. Everybody in the neighborhood knows who I am. But I don't know who you are. Do you go to Barker Street School?

LITTLE GHOST. I don't go to school.

ELSIE. How do you get by with that? Who are you? (*She pulls at the head of the* LITTLE GHOST.)

LITTLE GHOST. Ouch! Don't do that. It hurts.

ELSIE. Hurts? You're weird. What did you do—sew your costume to your head?

LITTLE GHOST. This isn't a costume.

ELSIE. What do you mean?

LITTLE GHOST. I might as well tell you. I'm a real ghost.

ELSIE. You're kidding.

LITTLE GHOST. No I'm not. I belong to *The Benevolent Society of Spooks and Spellcasters*. At least, I guess I do.

ELSIE. I still say you're fooling me. There aren't any ghosts.

LITTLE GHOST. I think I can prove it. Ludlillian said—no matter—just look into my eyes.

ELSIE. (*looks in the ghost's eyes*) Wow!

LITTLE GHOST. (*not knowing what she would see*) What do you see?

ELSIE. Nothing. I don't see anything at all. Just holes. (*She moves away from him.*) That's creepy.

LITTLE GHOST. So that's what Ludlillian meant. It is kind of creepy.

ELSIE. I think I'm afraid of you.

LITTLE GHOST. I wouldn't hurt a fly.

ELSIE. I don't think you would, and you don't act scary. I was even beginning to like you. But a real ghost?

LITTLE GHOST. Ludlillian says we're the good guys. Well, she isn't too good to Lilly, but she isn't really bad either. Anyhow you sure don't have to be afraid of me. I'm the one with the problem. I've got to get back to the gate by midnight and . . .

ELSIE. Like Cinderella. What happens if you don't? Do you turn into a pumpkin? (*She laughs.*)

LITTLE GHOST. Worse than that I think. But nobody told me. Ludlillian said I could take a souvenir back with me too, but I don't have one yet. Besides, I'm not sure I know the way back.

ELSIE. Why don't I go with you? It might be easier if there were two of us. And I could be your souvenir.

LITTLE GHOST. I'd rather have you as a friend. But I'd sure be glad to have company. What's your name?

ELSIE. Elsie. What's yours?

LITTLE GHOST. I don't seem to have one. Ludlillian calls me "kid."

ELSIE. That's good enough. Come on, kid, let's go. I'll have a great adventure and my sister will be jealous. It serves her right. (*They exit together left.*)

(*The curtain opens on the assembly hall as it was before. The gate still stands open.*)

THE VOICE OF LUDLILLIAN. (*from offstage*) I'm sorry, Lilly. I'm truly sorry. I need you.

(*Onstage* LILLY *manages to knock the top box off and then lift the other one enough to allow her to squeeze out from under her trap. Returning members of the society are already drifting in. It is almost midnight, and there is conversation about their souvenirs and their experiences. One goblin carries a large pumpkin, another a basket of apples. One of the elves looks comical in a Spanish shawl and one wears a cowboy hat. They are all excited and pay no attention to* LILLY *who moves to the gateway just as* LUDLILLIAN *enters.*)

LUDLILLIAN. There, you see I made it, Lilly. And I have my proper hat.

LILLY. (*falls into close step right beside* LUDLILLIAN *as they come downstage*) You know I am very annoyed with you.

LUDLILLIAN. You have every right to be. But I said I was sorry, and I admitted I need you. I might not have made it if I hadn't concentrated on my conscience. (*changes the subject*) I wonder where the kid is.

LILLY. You should have thought of him sooner. (*She looks toward the gateway as the* LITTLE GHOST *enters with* ELSIE.) But you're in luck. Here he is.

LUDLILLIAN. (*rushing to welcome him*) I'm sorry I left you alone, kid, but you got back and on time. I knew you could do it.

LITTLE GHOST. I don't think I could have without Elsie.

LUDLILLIAN. (*notices* ELSIE *for the first time*) Who's this?

LITTLE GHOST. Just who I said—Elsie.

LILLY. (*looking* ELSIE *over*) I think Elsie's trouble.

LITTLE GHOST. Why? She wanted to come back with me and . . .

LUDLILLIAN. (*who has also been inspecting* ELSIE, *interrupts*) She isn't one of us!

LITTLE GHOST. No, she's my souvenir.

LUDLILLIAN. You can't bring a person back here.

LITTLE GHOST. Why not?

LUDLILLIAN. A person doesn't belong here—can't live here —and I mean *live*. You've done a wrong thing, kid, and that's a transgression! If The Envoy sees her you'll go down the dark road and across the river and Elsie will die.

ELSIE. I don't think I'd like that. Besides, I thought this was just a kind of scavenger hunt. I have to get back home. I have a history test tomorrow and I wouldn't want to miss that.

LITTLE GHOST. What can we do?

LUDLILLIAN. It isn't quite midnight. She will have to get out of here before The Envoy comes back. Go on home, little girl, go home. (*She pushes her toward the gateway.*)

ELSIE. But we came a long winding way. I can't get there alone.

LUDLILLIAN. Then the kid will have to take you.

LILLY. You can't send him back *Out There.* He couldn't make it in time. Besides, you're the one to blame.

LUDLILLIAN. That's not true. I gave him a copy of the treaty. If he'd read it like I said to . . .

LITTLE GHOST. But I tried to tell you, Ludlillian, I can't read.

LUDLILLIAN. (*throws up her hands aghast*) Everything happens to me. (*She paces the floor with her head in her hands.* LILLY *still keeps step immediately behind her and now puts her arms around* LUDLILLIAN's *waist.*) OK. I'll take her.

LITTLE GHOST. If there isn't time for me, is there time for you?

LUDLILLIAN. I can cut some corners, and if I can get her to the crossroads she can find her way. Anyhow, it *was* my fault.

LITTLE GHOST. (*to* ELSIE) I'm sorry it worked out this way.

ELSIE. That's all right. I've had a wonderful adventure even if no one will believe me. Good-bye, kid.

LITTLE GHOST. Good-bye.

LUDLILLIAN. Don't waste what time there is. Let's go. (*She takes* ELSIE *by the hand and exits.* LILLY, *of course, goes*

with them—her arms still around LUDLILLIAN'S *waist.*
The LITTLE GHOST *steps off by himself, avoiding the*
others, but he keeps his eye on the gateway. TROLL
enters and moves through the crowd, stopping to ad-
mire a souvenir or make a comment. THE ENVOY *also*
enters, his face again shielded by the hood. There is a
general hubbub, and finally TROLL *goes to his make-*
shift desk. Everyone turns to him.)

TROLL. It is just about midnight. (*He checks his watch.*)
Is everyone ready for the countdown?

LITTLE GHOST. No, wait! Ludlillian's not here.

TROLL. (*looks around*) Ludlillian! I knew it would happen
sometime. Well, I'm sorry for her, but we can't wait.
Ten—nine—eight . . .

THE ENVOY. You can see she won't make it. Close the gate!

TROLL. Seven—six—five—four—three—two—(*He hesitates.*)
One. Close the gate!

(*The gate is no sooner closed than* LUDLILLIAN *ar-*
rives and shakes the bars.)

THE ENVOY. (*with delight*) You can let her in. I'm ready
for her. She is mine now.

(*The gate is opened again and* LUDLILLIAN *enters.*
LILLY *is no longer with her. She is now a part of*

her. *The white witch's hat sits on* LUDLILLIAN'S
head.)

LITTLE GHOST. (*runs to her*) If it hadn't been for me this
wouldn't have happened.

(THE ENVOY *puts a rope around* LUDLILLIAN'S *waist
in order to lead her away.*)

LUDLILLIAN. Forget it, kid. There comes a time when you
have to pay the piper.

TROLL. I don't know what you're talking about, but that
sounds like something Lilly would say. Where is Lilly?
What have you done with her?

LUDLILLIAN. Lilly? There is no Lilly. (*She taps her white
hat.*) She finally got into my head. (*to the* LITTLE
GHOST) Elsie sent this to you as a souvenir. (*She hands*
ELSIE'S *red bow to him.*) It will remind you of her—and
of me too.

TROLL. I take back what I said, Ludlillian. You do not belong across the river. I feel very sad.

LUDLILLIAN. To tell the truth, *I* feel better than I ever have.

LITTLE GHOST. (*clings to* LUDLILLIAN *and speaks to* TROLL)
Can't you do something?

TROLL. I wish I could.

LITTLE GHOST. If you can't, then let me go with her.

LUDLILLIAN. Look, kid, what would be the point? I did it to save you.

THE ENVOY. That's enough talk. Let's go.

TROLL. (*who has been poring over his papers*) Wait! There's something here in fine print at the end of the treaty.

THE CROWD. The fine print is always important.

TROLL. (*reads*) "If the offender is willing to go . . .

THE CROWD. She is. We attest to that.

TROLL. ". . . and does it to save someone else . . .

LITTLE GHOST. I'll attest to that.

TROLL. (*still reading*) ". . . said offender . . ."

LITTLE GHOST. Does it say she doesn't have to go after all?

TROLL. No, but it does say the offender must be returned by *The Malevolent League* the following Halloween. That's only a year!

LITTLE GHOST. A year's a long time.

LUDLILLIAN. It's not as long as forever, kid. Besides, even when you finally square yourself with your conscience, you can't expect to go scot-free. Don't worry about me.

I'll be back. (THE ENVOY *pulls her to the gateway but she turns just before they exit.*) And while I'm gone, kid, for goodness sake learn to read!

(*quick curtain*)

PRODUCTION NOTES

Since *Ludlillian and the Dark Road* is a play for Halloween, it isn't surprising that the costumes are half the fun. At the very outset, in the scene in front of the curtain, there is a parade of Halloween characters—a perfect opportunity to satisfy all those who want to be in the show but don't want to learn lines. Furthermore, these characters can turn up again in the assembly hall of *The Benevolent Society* and in the street scene *Out There*. Make the most of the situation.

The costumes of Lilly, Ludlillian, and the Little Ghost are well defined in the script, and the same is true of The Envoy. Just remember the devil mask and, by all means, the monk mask, the rope belt, and the chain and cross which change Wocan's representative from one character to another. No costume is described for Troll. Let your imagination have full sway.

In the street scene, we meet The Girl with the Beauteous Hat. She is a Southern belle, a Scarlett O'Hara, give her a hoop skirt and petticoats as well as the fancy chapeau. Don't forget Elsie's ghost costume is in two pieces so that the head covering can be removed. Also the red ribbon bow is important because Elsie sends it back to the Little Ghost for a souvenir. Then there's the rabbit, but you can always find a bunny suit around at Halloween. The props are relatively easy to provide. The sign, *The Benevolent Society of Spooks and Spellcasters,* can be printed on shelf paper or cardboard. A large notebook will serve as Troll's ledger, and he must have an envelope that he can give to Ludlillian—her assignment. You will need a copy of the treaty which Ludlillian takes from her shopping bag, and you will need shopping bags for both the witches. The rope The Envoy uses to lead Ludlillian away can be the same one he wears around his waist as the monk.

You will also need balloons, trick-or-treat sacks, a wand, and the souvenirs. A Spanish shawl, a pumpkin, apples, and a cowboy hat are the souvenirs mentioned in the script, but you can make substitutions to suit your fancy. Incidentally, the Southern belle will be happy to be provided with plenty of bubble gum.

Staging shouldn't be difficult. The front of the curtain scene at the opening requires only good direction. The dialogue and action of the characters must arouse and maintain interest and establish the tempo of the play. Ludlillian's teasing of the Little Ghost will provide movement.

The assembly hall scene is extremely simple. There must be a gate, of course, but it can be freestanding, not set in a wall. The script says Ludlillian rattles the bars, but it could be a solid gate just as well. Check the script to see if any changes in business or lines would result. Fashion a padlock out of heavy cardboard, and make it a big one.

It would be fine to have a backdrop for the street scene. Then when you make the scene change—and you haven't much time for it—you might not have to move the gate. Just push the boxes offstage. That will take only a matter of minutes. If you don't have a backdrop, just push the gate into the wings along with the boxes. Cardboard packing cartons are easily obtainable from furniture stores. Make certain one of them is big enough to cover the trapped Lilly.

Two other points should be mentioned. The first has to do with time. If you feel more of it should elapse for Lud-lillian to get Elsie safely on the road to her home and then return to the assembly hall, Troll's stage business could be expanded. He could take longer checking on the returning members of the society and looking at their souvenirs. The second point is one that should perhaps have been brought up in the beginning. The name, *Ludlillian.* Pronounce it slowly, emphatically, distinctly, so that the audience will hear it. It is a mouthful of a name, but that rascal of a witch simply turned up in the play with that moniker and nothing could be done about it. You may get to like her in spite of it, or just possibly because of it.

ARIZONA PILGRIMS

ARIZONA PILGRIMS

Characters

GLORIA TOBLE, ABOUT SEVENTEEN
JACK OGDEN, IN HIS EARLY TWENTIES
BILLY OGDEN, JACK'S BROTHER, ABOUT NINE
JAMISON PECK, RETIRED LOS ANGELES BUSINESSMAN
MARTHA PECK, HIS WIFE
DAN COCHRAN, A PILOT WHO OWNS AND OPERATES AN
    AIRLINE SERVICE
JOE RAMIREZ, A RANCHER

THE TIME: *Midmorning of Thanksgiving Day*
THE PLACE: *Somewhere in the desert area west of Phoenix.
The scene is laid in a kind of shed which looks as though
it has been abandoned. There is an old wooden table at
center stage, a couple of packing crates, a dilapidated
chair, and against the right wall is an army cot. Hanging
from a nail above the cot is a coil of heavy rope. The window off-center to the left in the back wall has a part of
the glass pane broken out, and the door on the left wall is
minus a bottom hinge.*

*As the curtain opens, the stage is empty and all that is
heard is the sound of the sandstorm outside. The door is
pushed open and* GLORIA *virtually blown in. She is casually
dressed, has a long scarf or muffler wrapped around her
neck, wears sunglasses, and holds a sweater up over her
head as protection against the storm. She looks about with
a critical eye, then throws her sweater down on one of the
crates and sits on the edge of the table.*

GLORIA. Well, this is certainly a mess.

> (JAMISON *and* MARTHA PECK *enter through the still
> open door, followed by* JACK *and* BILLY OGDEN.
> MARTHA *carries an overnight case held secure with
> a cord, and* JACK *carries a couple of books.*)

MARTHA. (*in an effort to get her breath*) It's good to get
out of that wind.

> (JACK *closes the door with difficulty because of the
> wind. Leaving his books on the table, he crosses
> right.* BILLY *follows close behind him.* JAMISON
> *seems to be exhausted from the exertion and heads
> for the chair.*)

BILLY. (*looking around with delight*) Boy, this is neat.

GLORIA. Neat! Kid, you must be sick.

BILLY. (*ignoring her*) Make a great clubhouse, wouldn't
it, Jack?

JACK. (*obviously a fellow of few words*) Right, Billy.

MARTHA. (*who hovers over her husband*) At least this is
better than sitting in the plane. (*to* JAMISON) Are you
all right, Jamison? (JAMISON *doesn't answer in words
but waves her off in a gesture indicating he is all right—
not to make an issue of it.*)

GLORIA. (*getting off the table and walking around*) I sure don't like the idea of being stranded here.

MARTHA. Maybe we won't be. We'll have to see what Mr. Cochran says.

GLORIA. There was some trouble with at least one of the engines. We could hear that.

MARTHA. Maybe he can fix it and we can go on again.

GLORIA. He's a pilot, not a mechanic. And even if he could fix it, nobody'd be able to get a plane off the ground in this weather. (*to* JACK) Where is he, anyhow?

JACK. He was still working with the radio.

> (*There is a sound at the door and* COCHRAN, *also with the wind at his back, is practically swept into the shed. His arms are loaded down with a flight bag, a first aid kit, maps and other odds and ends from the plane, all of which he deposits near the entrance before closing the door.*)

COCHRAN. I'm afraid the news is bad. Communication seems to be cut off. I don't even know whether my last message got through. We'll probably have to wait out the storm.

GLORIA. You mean we're not going to get to Phoenix for Thanksgiving after all? That's hilarious. I didn't want to go in the beginning, but even Phoenix would be better than this.

COCHRAN. I'll agree with that. Well, you've all met on the plane, but you may as well settle down and get better acquainted. Who knows how long we'll be here?

GLORIA. No reason to get chummy just because we turned up on a small plane together.

MARTHA. No need to be unfriendly either. After all, it is Thanksgiving.

JAMISON. (*finally having recovered enough to enter into the conversation*) Thanksgiving! Nobody even knows what Thanksgiving means anymore.

> (BILLY *has been wandering around the shed exploring in the corners, and he has discovered something that interests him downstage underneath the edge of the cot.*)

BILLY. Hey, look at all these ants. They're giant.

> (JACK *sits on the cot and idly watches with* BILLY.)

GLORIA. (*to* COCHRAN) Won't somebody realize the plane is down and try to find us?

COCHRAN. In time. When air control in Phoenix doesn't hear from us and we don't come in. But I'm not sure anybody can get to us until the weather clears. You can't see two feet in front of your face out there.

JAMISON. Where are we?

COCHRAN. Less than a hundred miles southwest of Phoenix, I'd say. (*He takes a map from his pocket and spreads it on the table.*) Right about here. (*He indicates the place on the map.*) Pretty much in the desert, but maybe not too far from Palo Verde. Of course, Palo Verde isn't very big.

BILLY. (*who is listening even though he seems to be engrossed in his ants*) Palo Verde. You know that town, don't you, Jack?

JACK (*quietly to* BILLY) Sure, but that doesn't get us there.

MARTHA. It doesn't really matter where we are if no one can reach us. We might as well make the best of things. It might be interesting to know why each of us decided to take a private plane to Phoenix on Thanksgiving morning.

GLORIA. It certainly wasn't my idea. My father called me yesterday afternoon and said I had to come. No way could I get a seat on a commercial flight. Someone at the school sent me to Mr. Cochran here. They told me he'd make the trip if he could get other passengers.

MARTHA. Phoenix is your home then?

GLORIA. Home? If you could call it that. There's just my
father. He sends checks, but I don't see him very often.

MARTHA. Jamison and I are on our way to visit our daughter and her family in Scottsdale. We didn't think we'd
go at first. Jamison wasn't feeling well and . . .

JAMISON. (*interrupting*) You aren't going to blame me for
not getting tickets earlier, Martha. You were the one
who thought we ought not to go.

MARTHA. I don't deny that, but you know you had a bad
cold last week. I'm still not sure we should have come,
and now look what's happened.

JAMISON. At least you can't say this was my fault. (*Wanting to divert the dialogue from himself, he directs a
question to* JACK.) How about you, young fellow? And
the boy? Brothers, are you?

JACK. (*looks up from watching the ants*) Yes.

BILLY. We're going to visit our grandfather . . .

JACK. (*interrupting and speaking to* BILLY *rather than to
the others*) Great-grandfather, Billy.

BILLY. Yeah, *great*-grandfather. He's awful old. He wanted
to see us and dad said we ought to go, because there
are so many things he can tell us about the old days
when the Indians . . .

JACK. They're not interested in all that, Billy. Go on back to your ants.

COCHRAN. You know my reason for the flight. It's just my job. Like the young lady said, if I can get passengers, I'll fly most anywhere. As a rule, my business comes when people can't get on the regular flights, and that's often on holidays.

GLORIA. Now that we've taken roll, what's the next boring thing we can do?

MARTHA. We could talk about Thanksgiving.

JAMISON. Humph! The significance of the day's been lost. Nobody believes in it.

MARTHA. You've already said that.

GLORIA. I believe in it. We get out of school.

JAMISON. Exactly. That's all it means to you.

BILLY. (*looks up from his ants again*) We always have a big dinner with pumpkin pie and turkey.

JAMISON. There you are. Food! No thought about that first Thanksgiving. And now some harebrained professor says they don't even tell it right in school. He says that there is no evidence of prayers being said, that the settlers wore bright colors and none of those big buckled shoes, and that they probably didn't even have turkey. Those wild turkeys, he says,were too hard to catch.

BILLY. The Indians could catch them.

MARTHA. Don't start on the subject, Jamison. You get so upset.

JAMISON. It's something to get upset about. I don't like my history disturbed.

COCHRAN. But if the story was wrong, it should be corrected.

JACK. Well, there's one part of the story you can count on. The Indians were there.

BILLY. That's right. My teacher said maybe nobody at Plymouth would have lived to celebrate Thanksgiving if it hadn't been for the Indians—especially Squanto. He liked the Englishmen, showed them how to plant corn and trap animals.

MARTHA. At any rate, I don't think Thanksgiving has to be for remembering how it was in 1621. The story of the Pilgrims is fine but . . .

JAMISON. (*interrupting*) That's another thing. This professor says they didn't even call themselves Pilgrims, and I say that's poppycock.

MARTHA. Don't interrupt me, Jamison. Thanksgiving is a time to be grateful for all things in our lives. When I was a little girl, we sat around the table after we'd stuffed ourselves, and each person had to tell what he was thankful for.

COCHRAN. We haven't had a chance to stuff ourselves, but we could still hear what the six of us have to say. It would help to pass the time.

GLORIA. You can skip me. Right now in this place I can think of nothing, nothing at all.

MARTHA. I'm thankful for so many things—my health, my family . . . It would take me hours to list everything.

JAMISON. I'm thankful that I won't be around when all of our traditions have been thrown out.

COCHRAN. I'd have something to be really thankful for if I could figure a way to get us into Phoenix.

JACK. I think we can all be grateful that the plane came down in one piece—thanks to Mr. Cochran.

MARTHA. I'll second that. (*to* BILLY) How about you, sonny?

BILLY. Well, I'd be glad if I had something to eat. I'm starving.

COCHRAN. That I can remedy. No pumpkin pie, but there are sandwiches and coffee and soft drinks on the plane. (*to* JACK) If you'll give me a hand, we'll get them.

(JACK *and* COCHRAN *open the door to leave and there is a strong gust of wind.* BILLY *tries to shield his ants.*)

BILLY. Hey! Watch it. This one guy here's having enough trouble as it is.

COCHRAN. (*laughs*) Sorry, kid, but what's more important to you—your empty stomach or those ants? (*He and* JACK *exit, pulling the door closed behind them.*)

JAMISON. (*who has come over to join* BILLY, *now stoops down beside him*) That is a big fellow there. What's he carrying?

BILLY. Whatever it is, it's bigger than he is.

JAMISON. Looks like a piece of bread.

MARTHA. (*perks up when she hears the word "bread"*) Where would he get bread? This place looks as though it's been abandoned for years. (*She comes to look at the ants, which seem to be making slow progress toward the window.*)

BILLY. Don't step on them. I want to see where they're going—especially that biggest one.

JAMISON. Maybe this shed isn't abandoned after all. Maybe it just looks that way because of the sand that's swept in here. That's sure a piece of bread he's carrying.

MARTHA. Hmmm. That puts a different light on things.

GLORIA. (*who has stayed at the table, now becomes interested in the conversation*) Why? What's so important about it?

MARTHA. If this shed is currently being used, there's probably a ranch house near here.

GLORIA. (*even more interested*) If that's so, maybe someone saw our plane come down.

JAMISON. In this blinding sand? I doubt that. Still, if there's a house maybe we could get to it. We might be able to contact Phoenix. I'd like to let the kids know we're all right.

MARTHA. (*to* GLORIA) And I'm sure your father will be worried.

GLORIA. (*shrugs*) I suppose. (*There is a sudden banging against the door.*) What's that?

MARTHA. It's probably the boys come back with their arms loaded. (BILLY *jumps up and goes with* MARTHA *and* GLORIA *to the door, but* JAMISON *doesn't move as fast and struggles to get to his feet.*) Just stay where you are, Jamison. We can manage. (*She and* GLORIA *pull the door open, but it is not* COCHRAN *and* JACK *outside. Instead a large barrel tumbles into the shed.*)

GLORIA. Where did that come from?

MARTHA. Let's get the door closed again. (*As they get behind it to push,* BILLY *looks out into the wind.*)

BILLY. It's sure taking them a long time. I'm going out to
help.

GLORIA. Don't be a dope, kid.

JAMISON. (*shouts from across the room*) No! No! Wait!
Don't do that, boy. (*But* BILLY *is already out the open
door.* JAMISON, *who is now on his feet, joins* MARTHA
and GLORIA.) Martha, why didn't you stop him?

MARTHA. How could I? He took us by surprise. He was out
the door before we realized what he was doing. Should
we go after him?

JAMISON. (*calls out the door*) Billy! (*to* MARTHA) We'd
just make matters worse if we went out there. (*calls
again*) Billy, come back.

GLORIA. It's only a little way to the plane. His brother will
see him.

JAMISON. I suppose you're right, but I don't like it. (*He
looks out into the storm hoping to catch sight of* BILLY.
The wind blows in, in spurts, but JAMISON *leaves the
door open.*)

GLORIA. All because of that stupid barrel.

JAMISON. (*Leaving his post at the door for a moment, he sets the barrel upright.*) The barrel isn't at fault, young lady. In a wind like this things have to be anchored down.

GLORIA. I just wish I hadn't come.

MARTHA. I don't mean to be nosy, my dear, but . . .

JAMISON. Yes, you do, Martha. Nosy is exactly what you mean to be.

MARTHA. Don't pay any attention to him. I'm just interested. I have a daughter of my own, you know. You said your father was all the family you had, dear? Your mother?

GLORIA. She died four years ago. We lived in Los Angeles then, and that's when dad put me in school and moved his business to Phoenix.

MARTHA. I'm sure he misses you.

GLORIA. I don't think he wanted me around. He never has any time for me. That old business of his. Toble Dynamics. Toble Dynamics. That's all he ever thinks about.

MARTHA. (*with surprise*) Toble? Are you saying you're Matthew Toble's daughter?

JAMISON. (*who is still keeping watch at the door interrupts with a shout*) Here they are. The boy's with them but . . .

(JACK *and* COCHRAN *enter.* JACK *is carrying* BILLY
*who has apparently been hurt. They don't seem to
be carrying anything else.* COCHRAN *closes the door
behind them.*)

JAMISON. What happened?

JACK. The plane door slammed shut on his ankle.

MARTHA. Oh dear, I feel it's our fault, but he ran out of
here before we could stop him.

GLORIA. I told him not to go.

JAMISON. We tried to call him back.

JACK. He said it was his own idea. You aren't to blame.

BILLY. I'm sorry. It was a dumb thing to do.

MARTHA. Bring him to the cot and we'll have a look. (JACK
crosses to the cot and puts BILLY *down.* COCHRAN *and*
JAMISON *follow along, but* GLORIA *hangs back.* MARTHA
takes off BILLY's *shoe and sock.*)

COCHRAN. I'm afraid we lost the food. We put the boxes
down to grab Billy, and the wind did the rest.

JAMISON. (*taking a look at* BILLY's *ankle*) That's a bad
bruise. Do you think it might be broken?

COCHRAN. We haven't really had a chance to look. (*He
does so.*) Well, I'm not sure.

JACK. How does it feel, Billy? Does it hurt?

BILLY. Not if I don't move it.

MARTHA. (*to* GLORIA, *who has been standing back at the table obviously not enjoying this kind of situation*) Will you hand me the first aid kit? I think Mr. Cochran put it there by the door when he first came in. (GLORIA *brings the kit to* MARTHA *but turns away again quickly.*) I wish we had some water to clean away the sand.

JACK. We really ought to try to get help.

COCHRAN. How? To go out into that just aimlessly (*motions toward the door*) would be asking for more trouble.

JACK. But this storm could last a couple of days.

GLORIA. We think we're near a house. The kid's ant is carrying a chunk of bread.

BILLY. Hey! How about my ant? How's he doing? Look and see. (GLORIA *goes to check.*)

COCHRAN. Even if we are near a house, we don't know in which direction.

GLORIA. (*finds the big ant now halfway to the window*) He didn't blow away, and he's moving right along— heading for the wall over by the window.

BILLY. Could somebody pull the cot around a little so I could watch him? (JACK *does so.*)

JAMISON. Wait a minute. The barrel.

JACK. What are you talking about?

JAMISON. The barrel. It blew against the door. That was when Billy ran out. If the barrel came from the house, and it must have, wouldn't the wind have brought it in a direct line.

COCHRAN. Yes, I suppose it would have. If we headed in a straight line into the wind . . . That's a thought. It's a long shot, but I'm willing to try it.

JACK. I'll go with you. It would be better with two of us, and I've been in sandstorms before.

BILLY. Dumb old ankle. I wish I could go.

GLORIA. You're the reason they're going, kid.

JACK. If we're right, the house could be only thirty or forty yards away.

MARTHA. (*who is still fussing with* BILLY's *ankle*) But what if you're wrong? We'd be worse off with you two lost out there.

JAMISON. (*takes the rope from the wall*) I have an idea. Why don't you tie one end of this rope to the table here and then string it through the break in the window. You take the other end, and that way if you find nothing you can get back.

JACK. (*takes the rope and roughly judges its length*) There's probably close to a hundred feet here. Is there any way we can get a little more length? The more we have the better.

COCHRAN. Three of us have belts.

BILLY. I have one too, even if it isn't very long.

JAMISON. Every bit helps.

> (*They all contribute the belts and* JACK *adds them to the rope.*)

GLORIA. I think it's a hopeless idea, but you can have my scarf.

MARTHA. I just remembered. The latch broke on my travel case and I tied it with cord. (*She goes to get it and it is added to the line along with* GLORIA's *scarf.*)

GLORIA. None of this extra stuff is very strong.

JACK. We won't be pulling on it. It's just a security line back to the shed.

> (*They finish tying and securing the end of the line to the table and push the table up to the window.*)

JAMISON. Can you get around the shed to the window? Stick close to the side of the building.

GLORIA. I still think it's crazy.

COCHRAN. We could wait awhile. My last radio message might have gone through, and maybe they're already figuring out a way to get to us.

JACK. We can't be sure of that, and I'd like to have a doctor look at Billy's ankle as soon as possible. We should at least try. (*He goes to* BILLY.) You know I'll be all right. How about you?

BILLY. I'm OK. (*He watches as* JACK *and* COCHRAN *go to the door.*) If there's a house you'll find it.

MARTHA. Be careful.

JAMISON. Good luck.

 (JACK *and* COCHRAN *exit. The others push the door shut and then go to the window to wait for their appearance. When* JACK's *hand reaches through the broken pane,* JAMISON *gives him the line.* BILLY *raps on the glass and waves.*)

JAMISON. Billy can tend the rope and keep us posted. (*The cot has been pushed close enough to the table so that* BILLY *can reach the end of the line.*)

GLORIA. They could die out there in that sand.

BILLY. They'll be all right. Jack said so. He didn't tell you, but he's been down around here lots of times with my great-grandfather. He lives on the reservation. That's where we're going.

GLORIA. (*with surprise*) You're Indian?

BILLY. Sure, Pima. But I've never lived on the reservation.

GLORIA. Why didn't you tell us before?

BILLY. I started to, but Jack said you wouldn't be interested. (*He tugs gently on the line.*) They're all right. (*He goes back to watching the ant.*)

MARTHA. You're a fine boy, Billy. And we are getting to know each other after all. (*turns to* GLORIA) Which reminds me, you didn't have a chance to answer my earlier question, my dear. Is Matthew Toble your father?

GLORIA. What if he is?

MARTHA. (*turning to* JAMISON) Jamison, she's Toble's girl.

GLORIA. You know him?

MARTHA. I should say so—at least Jamison does.

JAMISON. Yes, I know your father—knew him well when he was in Los Angeles. It was in a business way, of course. I never met your mother, but Matt always had my greatest respect.

MARTHA. We were so sorry to hear about his trouble.

(GLORIA *reacts to this, but* JAMISON *speaks before she can say anything.*)

JAMISON. Martha!

MARTHA. I'm sure she knows about it, Jamison. Everybody does.

GLORIA. What are you talking about? What trouble?

JAMISON. Martha shouldn't have said anything. It's none of her business. (*He tries to change the subject.*) Check the rope again, Billy.

BILLY. (*pulls on the rope again*) They still have it. It's OK.

GLORIA. If you know something about my father, tell me.

MARTHA. Jamison is right. I shouldn't have said anything, but I just assumed you knew.

GLORIA. I don't know anything. My father treats me like a child.

MARTHA. Of course he treats you like a child, my dear. He loves you. You're his little girl. You'll always be his little girl.

GLORIA. I don't think I mean anything to him. But I have a right to know if there's trouble.

MARTHA. Yes—I would think so. (JAMISON *shakes his head and lifts his hand trying to stop her, but she waves him off.*) No, Jamison, I've said this much, I might as well finish. (*to* GLORIA) You must be fair to your father, my dear. It's that business of his—that business you dislike so. He's losing it.

GLORIA. What? Why didn't he tell me?

JAMISON. (*resigned to his wife's meddling and feeling he must put in a word to soften the blow*) I suppose he hoped it would all work out, and you wouldn't have to know. Maybe with luck it will in time, but right now . . . Things just went downhill after your mother died.

GLORIA. (*bitterly*) Well, happy Thanksgiving Day. We should go round again now that I have something I can really be grateful for. (*She turns away, moves downstage left, leans against the edge of the barrel in a kind of daze and speaks almost to herself.*) Why couldn't he tell me?

MARTHA. I'm so sorry. If I thought . . .

JAMISON. Leave her alone, Martha. We've said enough.

(During these last speeches, BILLY, *who is still tend-ing the rope, pulls it once more very gently and it comes loosely into his hands. It has apparently been dropped at the other end.)*

BILLY. Something's wrong! Look! *(He holds up the slack rope.)* Something's wrong!

(They all rush to the window as the curtain falls.)

(After a moment, the curtain rises again on the same scene. It is an hour later. GLORIA *still leans against the rim of the barrel at left stage lost in her own thoughts.* BILLY *is, of course, still on the cot.* JAMISON *is seated at the table and* MARTHA *paces the floor.)*

MARTHA. We shouldn't have let them go.

JAMISON. Come on, Martha, you know we had no say in the matter.

MARTHA. *(glances at* GLORIA *and looks pleadingly at* JAMI-SON*)* And I'm worried about her.

JAMISON. *(shaking his head)* She'll be all right. It takes a little time.

BILLY. Maybe they dropped the rope because they found the house?

JAMISON. I'm sure that's just what happened. Say, Sonny, we haven't checked on that ant for a long while. Let's have a look. (*He goes over to stoop down beside the window.*) Well, now he seems to be gone. There's still a little trail of smaller fellows going into a chink in the flooring. Your giant must have made it home with the bread.

BILLY. That wasn't just bread. It was his Thanksgiving dinner. (*At that moment there is the sound of a horn over the wind.*) Say, did you hear that? It's Jack. I know it is. (*They all look toward the door as it opens and* JACK *enters with a stranger. They are carrying a couple of picnic baskets.*) I knew you'd make it.

JACK. Everything's going to be just fine. This is Joe Ramirez —the owner of that barrel.

RAMIREZ. Glad to know all of you. (*The introduction is acknowledged and* JACK *keeps right on talking.*)

JACK. Cochran stayed at the house to keep in touch with the Phoenix airport. His last message did get through. They know where we are. Cochran also contacted your daughter (*He nods to* MARTHA.) and your father. (*He nods to* GLORIA, *who turns toward him at the mention of her father.*) As a matter of fact, your father will be coming out after you as soon as possible. We could go back to the house right away if you want to, but Mr. Ramirez says the storm's already letting up. He has an open truck, and it might be better to wait a bit. They got ahold of a doctor too, and he says an hour or so won't make any difference. We brought plenty of food and water, and after all, Billy is starved, isn't he?

MARTHA. Whatever you say is fine with me.

BILLY. I say let's eat.

JAMISON. (*to* JACK) I agree. And by the way, young fellow, you haven't talked that much since we left Los Angeles.

BILLY. Indians only talk when they have something important to say.

JACK. (*laughs*) I might have known Billy would tell you about us as soon as I was out the door, but that's OK.

MARTHA. We were so worried when the rope went slack.

JACK. We did jerk it a couple of times, trying to give you some kind of signal. I guess you missed it. We were right in front of the house by then.

BILLY. See, I was right.

> (RAMIREZ *has been setting food out on the table which he has even covered with a cloth, and* BILLY *is watching with eagerness.* GLORIA *moves in toward the group.*)

GLORIA. (*to* JACK) You say my father is coming after me?

JACK. As soon as they'll let him on the highway.

MARTHA. Now I think we all have something new to be thankful for.

RAMIREZ. Better come and eat. My wife wants only empty dishes returned.

BILLY. Oh boy, there's turkey and a pumpkin pie!

JACK. *And* a corn pudding, Billy. Mr. and Mrs. Ramirez are Papagos. You know they'd never forget the corn.

BILLY. It's just like the first Thanksgiving.

JAMISON. Right you are, my boy. We are pilgrims in a way—put down here in desert wilderness. And once again, there would be no celebration without the Indians.

(*Everyone crowds around the table and begins to partake of the feast as the curtain falls.*)

PRODUCTION NOTES

Perhaps because *Arizona Pilgrims* is a serious drama, it requires conventional staging in order to be effective. No attempt will be made to suggest presenting the play with anything less.

The set, however, is simple enough—three walls, a

broken window, a sagging door, an army cot, an old table and chair, and a couple of crates. Given these things, you can turn your attention to the storm. There would be no play without the storm. Perhaps you can find a wind machine or at least a fan, and come up with something to simulate the blowing sand.

The time is now, which simplifies the costuming. Except for Gloria's sunglasses, scarf, and sweater and the belts of the men, no clothing is mentioned in the script. Just keep in mind the locale—Arizona. The climate is moderate in November. Jamison and Martha are probably in their sixties and would dress befitting their age and position in life. Cochran is a pilot, and although his business is his own, he might wear some kind of a uniform. Jack is in his twenties, maybe a college student; Billy is a nine year old. Remember they are Indian; don't select fair-skinned blonds for the roles. Joe Ramirez is a rancher, but this is Thanksgiving. It is unlikely that he would be in work clothes. Incidentally, make him a little more "Indian" than Jack and Billy. His skin could be darker, his hair black, and he might even wear a cloth headband. That is not uncommon in the desert.

There are very few props—Jack's books, Martha's overnight case, which is tied with a cord, the first aid kit, a flight bag, maps and papers that Cochran brings from the plane, the rope, and the barrel. Don't worry about measuring the rope. Jack says it's probably close to a hundred feet, and they try to make it a little longer. Distances are all speculative. We are never told exactly how far it is to the house anyhow.

Please concentrate on developing the characters. Gloria

is a young cynic, Jack generally reserved and quiet, Billy exuberant, and Martha and Jamison a bit quarrelsome with each other. Reach for the humor whenever possible, and remember there is always interest in a group of strangers thrown together by chance.

Two other things should be mentioned about the production. You will have to let the audience know that the play does not end when Billy says something is wrong and the curtain falls. Either by announcement or by printed programs, it must be made clear that there is more to follow. Also, if you do have a program, note that Jack, Billy, and Ramirez are not identified as Indian in the list of characters. This is intentional. You wouldn't want this revelation at the outset.

Brushing away all the traditional fiction of the first Thanksgiving, there still remains the fact. A small number of the settlers at Plymouth survived and their survival was due for the most part to the aid of the friendly Indians. *Arizona Pilgrims* is dedicated to that bit of history.

THE GREATER
MIRACLE

THE GREATER MIRACLE

CHARACTERS

MARK KRAMER, TWELVE YEARS OLD

SHEILA KRAMER, HIS EIGHT-YEAR-OLD SISTER

GRANDPA KRAMER

CATHY BAYLOR, SHEILA'S FRIEND

THE CHARACTERS IN THE ENACTMENT OF HISTORICAL EVENTS WHICH LED TO THE FIRST HANUKKAH CELEBRATION

THE TIME: *The first day of Hanukkah in the current year.*
THE SCENE: *The den of the Kramer home which takes up only the front two-thirds of the stage. The exit to the hall and thus to the front door is at the left. The right exit leads to the rest of the house, and a backdrop or curtain which closes off the upstage area serves as one wall of the room. There is a lounge chair and ottoman at the right and other furnishings as desired. As the front curtain opens,* MARK *and* SHEILA *enter from the left. They have just come from school and are in a heated argument.*

MARK. You are so dumb, Sheila. And you never listen to anything I tell you.

SHEILA. You're not the boss of me, Mark Kramer, so mind your own business.

MARK. I never said I was the boss of you. I only said that was a stupid answer you gave Cathy Baylor on the way to school this morning.

SHEILA. Oh, you think you're so smart just because you're twelve years old.

MARK. (*shrugs*) You don't have to believe me. Ask grandpa.

SHEILA. What do you think I'm going to do? (*She hurries to the right exit and calls offstage.*) Grandpa? Are you home? (*turns back to* MARK) Besides, you didn't even hear everything I told Cathy.

MARK. I heard one thing she said—that she was going to give you a present.

SHEILA. So. You're just jealous.

MARK. I'm not either. Anyhow, what you said about Hanukkah was dumb. You'll find out I'm right. Grandpa'll tell you. (GRANDPA KRAMER *enters from the right in time to hear the last of* MARK's *speech.*)

GRANDPA KRAMER. Such a ruckus here? What's grandpa going to tell you, Sheila?

MARK. (*not giving* SHEILA *a chance to speak*) This girl at school said . . .

SHEILA. She isn't "this girl." She's my friend.

MARK. OK. This friend said she was so happy that Sheila had Hanukkah now, because she wouldn't feel bad about not having a Christmas tree, and Sheila said . . .

GRANDPA KRAMER. (*interrupting as he crosses to* MARK *who is still at left stage*) Wait a minute, Mark. This seems to be Sheila's story. Why don't you let her tell it? (*turns to* SHEILA) What was it you said to your friend, honey?

SHEILA. I told her I didn't just *now* get Hanukkah. We've been celebrating it all my life.

MARK. See. Isn't that a silly answer? All her life. Big deal. Eight years.

GRANDPA KRAMER. Well, she wasn't wrong about that, was she? I've been celebrating Hanukkah all my life too.

SHEILA. (*to* MARK) So there.

GRANDPA KRAMER. Of course the holiday's been with us for centuries—but always as a simple observance. In recent years it does seem that people outside the Jewish faith are more aware of it. Maybe that's what your friend meant. Did you tell her anything else?

SHEILA. Not until we could get away from him. (*She gives* MARK *a sharp look.*) Then I told her how we celebrate for eight days, that we light candles every night and even I get to light one. And I said mama always makes latkes and that we sing special songs.

GRANDPA KRAMER. I think you covered a good deal.

SHEILA. That wasn't all. I told about playing the dreidel game and getting presents.

MARK. Well, even if she did say all that, Hanukkah is more
than games and food and presents. Even more than
lighting the candles. Isn't that so, Grandpa?

GRANDPA KRAMER. Yes, that's so. In fact, our festival of
dedication must not become only an excuse for parties
and presents. I think Sheila knows that. She might not
understand the real meaning of the holiday—but give
her time.

SHEILA. Mama told me the story of the first Hanukkah, but
I just can't remember it all. She said it was enough for
now to know that we light the Hanukkah menorah to
remind us of some very brave people of long ago.

GRANDPA KRAMER. There, you see, Mark? But tell me,
since you find fault with Sheila's answers, what would
you tell her friend? We'll find out how well you've
learned your lessons. (*As he speaks, he crosses to right
stage and sits in the armchair.*)

MARK. (*pompously*) Well, I'd tell her that the celebration of Hanukkah, the Festival of Lights, is based on an
old legend. (*He speaks almost mechanically, reciting
the words he has committed to memory.*) When Judah
Maccabee and his followers returned to Jerusalem they
rebuilt and rededicated the Temple. Then they wanted
to light the altar lamp, and they found a small vessel of
unprofaned oil which had been closed with the seal of
the high priest and hidden away in the days of the
Prophet Samuel. Although there was only enough oil for

one day, it miraculously lasted for eight until new clean oil was obtained. (*He lets out a breath as he finishes his recital.*) And that is why we celebrate for eight days.

GRANDPA KRAMER. Oh, you have memorized the story well, and that is a lovely legend about the oil. But you know, Mark, there's another legend that says we celebrate for eight days because when the Jews reclaimed the Temple they found eight Syrian spears which they converted into a lampstand. (*He strokes his chin as though weighing the two theories.*) Hmmm. Which am I to believe? (*then as though making a great decision*) Perhaps it doesn't matter. The holiday doesn't hang on any legend. We must take into account the history.

SHEILA. See, smarty, you aren't always right.

GRANDPA KRAMER. It isn't a question of right and wrong, Sheila. It's just that folklore can't take the place of the historical origin of Hanukkah.

MARK. I know the history too, Grandpa. I've studied hard.

GRANDPA KRAMER. I know you have, and I'm sure you've learned that story by heart too, but when you repeat the words, Mark, do you feel something inside of you?

MARK. I don't know what you mean.

GRANDPA KRAMER. Then come here and sit down, both of you, and I'll try to explain. (SHEILA *settles herself cross-legged at her grandfather's feet, and* MARK *sits on the ottoman nearby. The footlights go off and a spotlight is trained on the three characters as* GRANDPA KRAMER *begins his story.*) Let's see now, where to begin . . . Certainly we'll have to go back over two thousand years, back to an ancient world. The Jewish people lived in the land which is now called Israel, and for a long, long time the Syrian-Greeks had been trying to make the Jews adapt to their ways. However, it was when Antiochus IV inherited the throne that things became very bad. This Antiochus was a tyrant—a cruel man. He worshiped idols, which was, of course, his right, but he insisted that all his subjects do the same. He banned Sabbath observance and Torah study and he put Greek statues in the Temple. Life in Jerusalem turned into a nightmare.

SHEILA. (*interrupting*) I know what a nightmare is—a bad dream.

MARK. Be quiet.

GRANDPA KRAMER. That's all right, Mark. It's good that Sheila can understand how dreadful it would be to *live* in a nightmare. The people in Jerusalem weren't dreaming. Antiochus patrolled the streets, broke into homes, and killed anyone who did anything that was Jewish. Some Jews said they'd do what he wanted. They didn't want to die. But many were killed, and others left Jerusalem hoping to live simple lives in the neighboring villages. Among those who left, there was a man,

Mattathias, who it is believed went to the village of Modi'in with his five sons.

(*The backdrop is raised to reveal the dimly lit scene of Mattathias's approach into Modi'in, and as* GRANDPA KRAMER *continues, the following action ensues in pantomime.*)

Well, Antiochus wasn't going to let these people alone, and he followed them, and when his soldiers came to Modi'in they could tell that Mattathias was the leader there, and they asked him to offer a sacrifice according to the king's decree. Mattathias refused, saying, "we will not obey the law of the king by departing from our worship . . ." Just then another Jew said he would do whatever the soldier asked, but before he had a chance to, Mattathias ran up and killed the man right there on the altar. Then he turned and killed the commander, and the villagers joined in and together they killed all the soldiers.

(SHEILA *buries her head in her hands as the pantomimed skirmish goes on for a few minutes after* GRANDPA KRAMER *stops speaking. Then the backdrop is brought down again and* SHEILA *lifts her head.*)

SHEILA. That's terrible, Grandpa. I don't like people to be killed.

MARK. Oh, you're such a baby.

GRANDPA KRAMER. Shush, Mark. (*to* SHEILA) The truth is often terrible, honey. You are right not to like killing, but at that time there was no other way. Mattathias and his family and followers decided they would have to fight, and so they fled to the hill country to hide out while they made plans.

MARK. They didn't have much to fight with.

GRANDPA KRAMER. No, and there were no big battles in the first year. There was sorrow though, for Mattathias died.

MARK. That was too bad, because he never saw the Temple rebuilt.

GRANDPA KRAMER. Yes, that was a shame, but before he died, Mattathias named his successors—his second son, Simon, and his third son, Judah. (*He breaks the tension of his story to direct a question to* MARK.) All right, Mark, with your good memory, what was it he said?

MARK. (*reciting again*) Simon, because "he is a man of counsels . . . shall be a father to you. Judah Maccabee, strong and mighty from his youth, will be your captain and will fight the battles of the people."

SHEILA. Judah the Maccabee. That's the one mama told me about. Maccabee was his nickname.

MARK. Grandpa, if Sheila doesn't keep still, you won't get to the rest of the story.

SHEILA. You interrupt as much as I do.

GRANDPA KRAMER. Don't squabble. And Sheila's right about Judah. It was by his nickname that the whole group became known—The Maccabees. And when Judah took over after his father's death, things picked up. They won victories in the face of big odds, and three years after they had fled from Jerusalem, they marched back into the holy city. Judah sent troops to fight off the soldiers stationed there, and then they went to the Temple. (GRANDPA KRAMER *heaves a deep sigh.*) What they found made them very unhappy. Everything was a shambles . . . (*He looks at* SHEILA *and changes the word.*) . . . a mess, Sheila. Yes, a mess, just like your classroom when the vandals broke into the school last spring. (*The backdrop goes up again and in the same dim light as before the outer courts of the Temple and the havoc there are visible—the gate half burned away, stones scattered, a table overturned, whatever possible to show the destruction.*) The gates were burned. Weeds had grown up in the courts and the chambers pulled down. Judah and his men fell to the ground and cried to heaven. (*Again there is pantomimed action to simulate the activity.*) Then they blew upon the trumpets and set to work to rebuild. "They took whole stones according to the Law, and built a new altar after the fashion of the former; and they built the sanctuary, and the inner parts of the Temple . . . and they brought the candlestick, the altar of burnt offerings and of incense, and the table, into the Temple . . . and finished all the works which they had undertaken." (*The inner parts of the Temple are offstage left and a steady procession of the Maccabees moves across to the exit, each man carrying his burden. Once more the backdrop falls into place and* GRANDPA KRAMER *finishes the story.*) And then they rose up early in the morning on the twenty-fifth of Kislev and, three years after the desecration of the Temple, they dedicated it anew. "Judah and his brothers and the whole congregation of Israel ordained that the days of the dedication of the altar should be kept in their season year by year for eight days, from the twenty-fifth of the month Kislev with gladness and joy."

(*The footlights go up again and the spotlight is turned off.*)

SHEILA. Nobody tells a story like you do, Grandpa.

GRANDPA KRAMER. I hope I have told it in a way you can understand. At any rate there is the history. There are, of course, links to older dedication observances. Moses had a ceremony when he built the Tabernacle in the desert, Solomon, too, when the first Temple was built, and the Jews who returned from the Babylonian Exile when they built the Second Temple. But the very word, Hanukkah, means dedication, and what makes it unique is the fact that it celebrates the rededication of the Temple *and of the human spirit.*

MARK. (*who has been listening attentively to the account of the rebuilding of the Temple seems puzzled*) I've read the story many times, Grandpa, and you do tell it better than it is in the books, but I'm not sure what I'm supposed to feel inside.

GRANDPA KRAMER. Then perhaps I've failed, but remember that the revolt led by Judah Maccabee marked a time— perhaps the first known time—that a people fought for their religious freedom. Fought, Mark, killed and were killed. And you said it, they had very little to fight with. The enemy, well armed and riding their majestic elephants, was advancing to destroy them—to destroy us, Mark. Think of yourself in Judah Maccabee's sandals and tell me then you feel nothing.

(MARK *says nothing but gets up from the ottoman and walks off to the left, deep in thought.*)

SHEILA. But if we're supposed to think about all that fighting, why do we get presents and play games and eat latkes and doughnuts?

GRANDPA KRAMER. Because Hanukkah is after all a holiday of gladness and joy. People always have fun when they're joyful. But we must be careful not to let gifts and food and games blot out the ideal of Hanukkah.

SHEILA. But, Grandpa, you're the one who gives us the Hanukkah gelt. And mama always has other little presents for us.

GRANDPA KRAMER. Simple things are fine. And how much do I give you—thirty-six cents in eight days. (*laughs*)

You're not going to be spoiled with that. (*He looks to* MARK.) Mark—are you all right?

MARK. (*turns thoughtfully to his grandfather*) I've been thinking. I don't know whether I could have fought like that. It makes me kind of sick to think about it.

GRANDPA KRAMER. Good. Then you do feel something, and as your years multiply your feeling will grow stronger. Don't forget . . . (*He is interrupted by the ring of the doorbell, and* MARK *and* SHEILA *both hurriedly exit left, trying to beat each other to answer the summons.*)

GRANDPA KRAMER. (*shaking his head, he mutters to himself.*) How fast I lose their attention, but I guess it is sometimes hard to understand the importance of a victory for religious freedom. I'll give him time too.

(MARK *reenters from the left.*)

MARK. It was Cathy.

(SHEILA *enters pulling her friend,* CATHY, *along with her.* CATHY *carries a gift-wrapped box.*)

SHEILA. This is my friend, Cathy, Grandpa. I wish she'd been here to hear the story. Cathy, this is my Grandpa Kramer.

CATHY. Pleased to meet you, Mr. Kramer. Sheila's always talking about you.

GRANDPA KRAMER. Saying good things I hope. Well, certainly any friend of Sheila is a friend of mine.

CATHY. I can't stay, but my mother said I could give Sheila a Hanukkah present. (*She proffers the package.*) I hope you like it.

SHEILA. Gee, thanks, Cathy. What is it? (*She takes the package.*)

CATHY. I'm not going to tell, but my mother picked it out. I'd better go now. Dinner's about ready at home.

GRANDPA KRAMER. Well now, you come again when you can stay longer, young lady.

CATHY. I will, thanks. (*She turns to leave and* SHEILA *puts the package on a convenient table and starts to accompany her friend to the door.* CATHY *speaks to* SHEILA *as they exit.*) I'll see you tomorrow, Sheila.

MARK. (*looks at the box*) Are you going to let Sheila keep that?

GRANDPA KRAMER. Why not?

MARK. Because you said we shouldn't get presents.

GRANDPA KRAMER. Now, I didn't say exactly that.

> (SHEILA *runs back into the room and tears off the wrappings of the package.*)

SHEILA. I wonder what it is. (*She pulls out a ceramic elephant bank and holds it up.*) A bank to hold my gelt, Grandpa. Isn't it a nice present? But I don't have anything for Cathy. I should give her a present too.

GRANDPA KRAMER. You can ask your mother, but I don't think you need to. Instead, why not invite your friend over tomorrow night when we light the candles, and maybe she can stay for dinner.

SHEILA. That'll be good. And you can tell the story all over again.

GRANDPA KRAMER. (*laughs*) I don't know about that. (*He picks up the bank and turns it around in his hands, noting the sticker on the side.*) Say, this was made in Israel. Very thoughtful of Cathy's mother.

MARK. (*who has been sulking*) I think you ought to give it back.

SHEILA. Mark's just mad, Grandpa, because he didn't get anything.

MARK. That's a lie. Grandpa's just been telling us we shouldn't be thinking of presents at Hanukkah—that we should have feelings about the Jews fighting for freedom.

GRANDPA KRAMER. I'm not sure I need to tell you anything about fighting—either one of you two. I seem to have given you an idea of the importance of Hanukkah, but I don't seem to be able to do anything to make you get along together. It worries me to see you bickering all the time.

SHEILA. Don't worry about that, Grandpa. Daddy says we're normal.

GRANDPA KRAMER. Well, let me settle this right now, Mark. Sheila should keep the present *and* keep her friend. Cathy and her mother put thought and consideration into that gift. It was from the heart. And an elephant— they even gave something that recalls the very event we celebrate.

SHEILA. Mama and I made elephant cutouts yesterday to put up in the window.

MARK. That's another thing. I don't see why we have elephants at Hanukkah anyhow. Decorations, cookies. It was the enemy who used the elephants against us.

GRANDPA KRAMER. But we won, Mark, we won. And just remember that for twenty-one centuries the Hanukkah flames have been lit, flames which reflect the glow of that Maccabee victory.

MARK. OK, so we light the candles to remind us of the victory. Then tell me this. Why do we bother with the legend of the oil at all?

GRANDPA KRAMER. That's a good question. And it brings us right back where we started. You see, Mark, legends are as revealing as history in the understanding of our holidays. History tells us more or less what happened; legend explains what we feel about it. We need them both. It is all very well to believe that the oil, which should have lasted only one day burned for eight, but it is a poetic substitution for a greater miracle. I don't know of anything more miraculous than the survival— both physical and spiritual—of the Jewish people.

MARK. (*thoughtfully*) Nobody's explained it to me just like that before.

GRANDPA KRAMER. Then think on it. (*He looks at his watch.*) Well now, it's getting late. The sun is gone. (*He turns to gather his grandchildren to him.*) Come on, Sheila, it's time to kindle the lights. I think your mother will be ready for us. (*They exit right as the curtain falls.*)

PRODUCTION NOTES

The fact that no music is called for in *The Greater Miracle* should be mentioned at once. Although the play does not depend on Hanukkah hymns or chants, they would certainly add to the spirit of a holiday production. You might present either live or recorded music before the curtain goes up and again when it has come down, framing the play, so to speak. A choice of selections will probably be available to you; use whatever you feel is most appropriate.

As for the staging, the script calls for a backdrop or curtain to block off the upstage area. When it is lifted be sure that the light is dim. You want the pantomime action to be shadowy and veiled. If you have a traditional set, the curtain could open to reveal a picture window and the pantomime could be enacted beyond it. Or better yet, if you could have a translucent curtain you need not open it. Just use strong lights behind it. The time between the fighting scene and the Temple scene is short, but so little need be done to portray the destruction. It's mostly a matter of putting out an overturned table and a few cartons for toppled stones. Perhaps you can use painted flats to show the weeds and the burned gate. Do experiment with whatever facilities you have.

Except for the lounge chair, ottoman, and a table on which Sheila puts the present, you can set the stage as you wish. Be sure nothing interferes with the audience's view of the pantomime. Incidentally, if you put a table and a lamp beside the lounge chair you might not need the spotlight.

The time is the present, and Mark, Sheila, and Cathy would be dressed to fit your particular midwinter climate. Grandpa Kramer would also be in contemporary clothes. The Biblical figures would wear costumes of their day, and it should be no problem to find pictures in religious books.

You will need the wrapped gift box and a ceramic or papier-mâché elephant. It need not be a bank. No one will be able to see such a detail. You can add other small props if you wish—Mark and Sheila might, for example, carry books home from school, and Grandpa might have the local newspaper tucked under his arm when he enters. Don't forget the doorbell. None of the things mentioned in the scenes of the desecrated Temple or in the rebuilding needs be exactly as described. Remember the light is dim, the figures shadowy, and as long as the props suggest what is scattered about or carried across the stage, that is all that is necessary. It would be nice, though, to have the trumpet.

The movement of the play will probably be adequately maintained by the pantomime scenes, but if you want more action, Grandpa Kramer can get up and walk about as he tells the story. Again you can experiment.

The lines taken directly from the First Book of Maccabees are in quotes in the script. They can be put in simpler words if you wish. Such decisions are in the hands of the director.

If *The Greater Miracle* is presented for a mixed group, with religious and ethnic differences, you may want to explain more about the Jewish customs. You don't need to change the play, but perhaps you could have explanatory material in a printed program—the tradition of gelt, the dreidel game, the Hanukkah menorah, and why the shammash stands higher than the eight candles, is lit first, and is used to light the others. It might be a wonderful opportunity for an intercultural exchange.

WHAT WILL YOU TELL US OF CHRISTMAS?

WHAT WILL YOU TELL US OF CHRISTMAS?

CHARACTERS

THE CHORUS CELESTIAL, REPRESENTING THE SACRED ASPECT
OF CHRISTMAS, ANY NUMBER

THE CHORUS TEMPORAL, REPRESENTING THE SECULAR AS-
PECT OF CHRISTMAS, ANY NUMBER

THE CHILDREN OF TOMORROW, ANY NUMBER

THE PEOPLE IN THE STREET SCENE, THE SHOPPERS, THE
CHILDREN, THE CAROLERS

THE PEOPLE IN THE HOME SCENE, AS MANY AS DESIRED

THE TRADITIONAL CHARACTERS OF THE NATIVITY, JOSEPH,
MARY, THE SHEPHERDS, THE ANGEL, THE KINGS

*This is a combination of choral reading, tableaux, pag-
eantry, and pantomime presenting Christmas in all its
aspects from secular celebration to religious significance.
The choral readers are in three groups. The* CHORUS CELES-
TIAL *is robed in light blue. The* CHORUS TEMPORAL *is in
red. The* CHILDREN OF TOMORROW *are in white. It should
be noted that even though well-known carols figure in the
presentation, they are spoken, not sung. The curtain is
closed as the three groups take their places at the foot
of the stage—the* CHILDREN OF TOMORROW *between the
other two—and the program begins.*

CHORUS CELESTIAL. (*in soft, low tones*)

"Silent night, Holy night, All is calm, all is bright.
'Round yon Virgin Mother and child, Holy . . ."

CHORUS TEMPORAL. (*interrupting in sharp staccato rhythm*)
"Christmas is coming and the geese are getting fat
Please to put a penny in an old man's hat."

CHORUS CELESTIAL. (*still in low tones but introducing an element of persistence*)
"Holy infant so tender and mild, Sleep in heavenly peace,
Sleep in heavenly peace."

CHORUS TEMPORAL. (*still sharper*)
"Please to put a penny in an old man's hat—
Just a copper penny in a beggar's hat—
"Christmas is coming and the geese are getting fat."

CHORUS CELESTIAL. (*increasing now in intensity*)
"Come all ye faithful, Joyful and triumphant,
O come ye, O come ye to Bethlehem."

CHORUS TEMPORAL. (*louder now and gaining in momentum*)
"Deck the halls with boughs of holly, Fa la la la la la la la la."
(*One line or section of the group steps out toward the* CHORUS CELESTIAL *as though to push them out of focus —voices at a peak in the momentum.*)
"Don we now our gay apparel, Fa la la la la la la la la.
Troll the ancient Yuletide carol, Fa la la la la la la la la."

CHORUS CELESTIAL. (*now in rising, insistent tones*)
"Hark the herald angels sing, 'Glory to the newborn King!'"

CHORUS TEMPORAL. (*with shrill voices, interspersed with laughter*)
"Jingle bells, jingle bells, jingle all the way.
Oh what fun it is to ride in a one-horse open sleigh."

(*The* CHILDREN OF TOMORROW *have been listening, turning their heads from one group to the other as each spoke. Now they interrupt in high-pitched but smooth and steady voices.*)

CHILDREN OF TOMORROW.
Softly, softly. Stop the friction.
Let the rising discord cease.
You who speak of calm and holy
Why at odds with fatted geese?
Why do you who call for holly
Lift your voices—almost shout?
And with noisy bells ajangling
Seek to drown the others out?

CHORUS TEMPORAL.
Know you not about *our* Christmas
And the pleasure it will bring?

CHORUS CELESTIAL.
Know you not about *our* Christmas
And the birth of Christ the King?

CHILDREN OF TOMORROW.
Only rumors, faint and distant.
Only rumors have we heard.

Ah, but Christmas—Christmas—Christmas,
What a tantalizing word.

CHORUS CELESTIAL.
Why then do you come to chide us
Criticizing our dissent?

CHORUS TEMPORAL.
Who indeed are you to question?
What your purpose—your intent?

CHILDREN OF TOMORROW. (*Here the beat changes and there
is a rolling softness to the voices.*)
We are Tomorrow's Children
The legion of those yet unborn.
We come to learn about Christmas
And not to chide or to scorn.
But who can we trust to tell us
When you cannot seem to agree
On what the Yuletide stands for
Or what it will mean . . . (*Here a solo voice finishes
the line.*) to me?
(*Then two more solo voices echo one after the other.*)
and me? and me?

CHORUS TEMPORAL. (*eagerly*)
Choose us and we will show you
What a merry Christmas brings.
All the bustle and the planning
All the shining, gracious things.

CHORUS CELESTIAL. (*somberly*)
Oh stay—they will not tell you
Of shepherds and a star.

CHORUS TEMPORAL.
Pay no heed to what they're saying
Come along, it isn't far.

CHORUS CELESTIAL. (*turns aside in unison and speaks softly as in the beginning*)
"Silent night, Holy night, All is calm, all is bright."

CHORUS TEMPORAL. (*with a wide arm gesture to the stage as the footlights go on*)
There! The lights are beckoning
And everyone will share
In the festive celebration
There's excitement in the air.

CHILDREN OF TOMORROW.
There is promise of excitement
But that much rumor told.

CHORUS TEMPORAL.
Then wait! It's just beginning;
Watch the scenes as they unfold.

(*The curtain opens to reveal the street scene tableau. Only a shallow downstage area is used here with an appropriate backdrop. This allows for a later scene to be at least partially set up behind it.*)

There are spotlights focused on the SHOPPERS, *the* CAROLERS, *the* CHILDREN *in the window.*)

The shoppers hurry homeward
For the hour is getting late.
The children at the windows
Are impatient—they can't wait.
The carolers assembled
At the closing of the day
Sing of life and laughter
"Let nothing you dismay."
There is welcome on each threshold
A wreath upon each door . . .

CHILDREN OF TOMORROW.
And all of this is Christmas?

CHORUS TEMPORAL. (*lightly*)
All of this and so much more.

CHORUS CELESTIAL.
More—more—more.

(*The curtain closes on the street scene and a soft tolling of bells begins.*)

CHORUS TEMPORAL.
Attend! The bells are ringing
Melodic bells that say
They toll the morning's glory
They welcome Christmas day.

CHORUS CELESTIAL. (*in a plaintive tone*)
"I heard the bells on Christmas day
Their old familiar carols play,
And wild and sweet the words repeat
Of peace on earth, good will to men."

CHORUS TEMPORAL. (*The entire group takes a step forward
and leans toward the* CHORUS CELESTIAL.)
Don't try to find a message
In the chiming of the bells
They only ring for pleasure
As the merry clamor swells.

CHILDREN OF TOMORROW.
We follow where you lead us.
We hear just what you choose.
We see just what you show us,
But discord still pursues.

CHORUS TEMPORAL.
And there is more to show you
And more for you to hear.
A thousand things at Yuletide
To please the eye and ear.

CHORUS CELESTIAL. (*with a sadness*)
"Then pealed the bells more loud and deep
God is not dead, nor doth he sleep;
The wrong shall fail, the right prevail,
With peace on earth, good will to men."

CHORUS TEMPORAL.
Look indoors and see the promise
That the season will fulfill.
There's an atmosphere of friendship;
There's an aura of good will.

> (*The curtain opens on the full stage—the living room of a family home. At the back, off center to the left, is the Christmas tree, appropriately decorated and with packages scattered beneath it—most of them opened. Paper and ribbons are strewn about. To the right of the tree, perhaps in the corner, is a fireplace where the filled stockings are hanging. There is holly and other greenery arranged on the mantel, and mistletoe hangs at an entrance or from a chandelier if it is feasible to have one. Children play on the floor with toys and games. Father is asleep in an armchair at right center.*)

CHORUS TEMPORAL. (*continues*)
And behold in wondrous splendor
With a touch of majesty,
Adorned with lights and glitter,
Stands the radiant Christmas tree.

CHORUS CELESTIAL.
The star! It was forgotten
In the frenzy of elation.
The star! The very symbol
Of the holy celebration.

CHORUS TEMPORAL. (*rushing right on—the words seeming
to tumble over one another*)
And underneath the branches,
Scattered left and right,
Is evidence that Santa
Found his way here in the night.
There are stockings at the fireplace—
They bulge and sag with treats,
With candy canes and licorice
And other tempting sweets.
The family has gathered—
There's laughter and there's noise;
There is placid occupation;
There is squabbling over toys.
The mistletoe invites you
And the holly's strewn about . . .

CHILDREN OF TOMORROW.
There is also someone sleeping.

CHORUS TEMPORAL.
It is father—all worn out.
Soon now comes the feasting,
And when that is under way
All will toast a jolly Christmas
And a happy holiday.

CHORUS CELESTIAL.
No star. No star. No star.

CHILDREN OF TOMORROW.
A jolly, happy Christmas

Of frolic, feast and song.
Is this the sum and substance?
There must be something wrong.
Is there no deeper meaning?
What about the newborn King?
The star that guided shepherds?
And didn't angels sing?

CHORUS TEMPORAL.

We've no memory of shepherds
Or angels, we confess,
But as to depth of meaning,
What's wrong with happiness?

CHORUS CELESTIAL.

No memory of shepherds?
No recall of the thrill
Of heavenly voices echoing
"On earth peace to men of good will?"
Though you've told a part of Christmas,
If this is all you know
Then come with us in reverence
To a time long, long ago.

(*A small number of the* CHORUS CELESTIAL—*perhaps four or five—speak as one in a mystic prophetic tone and in prose.*)

THE SELECT GROUP. There went out a decree from Caesar Augustus that the whole world should be enrolled each in his own city. And Joseph also went up from Galilee out of the city of Nazareth into Judea. And with him was his wife Mary, and they found the city of David which is called Bethlehem overcrowded with travelers. There was no room for them at the inn.

CHORUS CELESTIAL—THE MAIN BODY.
No room at the inn. No room.
"O little town of Bethlehem!
How still we see thee lie;
Above the deep and dreamless sleep
The silent stars go by.
Yet in thy dark streets shineth
The everlasting Light;
The hopes and fears of all the years
Are met in thee tonight."

THE SELECT GROUP. Weary and cold they sought shelter in a simple stable. There Mary brought forth her firstborn son and wrapped him up in swaddling clothes and laid him in a manger.

CHORUS CELESTIAL—THE MAIN BODY.
"Once in royal David's city
Stood a lowly cattle shed,
Where a mother laid her baby,
In a manger for His bed."

THE SELECT GROUP. And this was Jesus the Son of God. And there were in the same country shepherds watching over their flock, and behold an angel of the Lord stood by them and the brightness of God shone round about them and they feared with a great fear. And the angel said to fear not for behold I bring you good tidings of great joy that shall be to all the people. For this day is born to you a Saviour who is Christ the Lord in the city of David.

CHORUS CELESTIAL—THE MAIN BODY.
"The first Noel the angel did say
Was to certain poor shepherds in fields as they lay;
In fields where they lay keeping their sheep,
On a cold winter's night—that was so deep
Noel, Noel, Noel, Noel—
Born is the King of Israel."

THE SELECT GROUP. And suddenly there was with the angel a multitude of the heavenly host praising God and saying Glory to God in the highest and on earth peace to men of good will.

CHORUS CELESTIAL—THE MAIN BODY.
"Angels, from the realms of glory
Wing your flight o'er all the earth;
Ye, who sang creation's story,
Now proclaim Messiah's birth."

THE SELECT GROUP. And when the angel departed the shepherds said let us go over to Bethlehem, and they went with haste and found Mary and Joseph and the infant and seeing, they understood. Now the night was bright with shining stars, but one star was brighter than all the rest and three wise men from the East were guided by it to where the newborn child was sheltered.

(*On this cue the* THREE KINGS *and their train of attendants approach the stage from the back of the theater.*)

CHORUS CELESTIAL—THE MAIN BODY. (*Speaking as the entourage moves onto the stage and exits into the wings. The curtain remains closed.*)
"We three kings of Orient are;
Bearing gifts we traverse afar,
Field and fountain, moor and mountain.
Following yonder star.
O star of wonder, star of night,
Star with royal beauty bright,
Westward leading, still proceeding,
Guide us to Thy perfect light."

THE SELECT GROUP. (*also speaking while the procession of the* KINGS *moves to the stage*) And they knelt before the Son of God and prayed. The whole stable was bright with the light of the star and there was great joy in Mary's heart and there was great joy in the world, for this was Christmas.

(*The curtain opens on the Nativity tableau, complete with the* SHEPHERDS *and the* WISE MEN.)

CHORUS CELESTIAL—THE MAIN BODY.
"Joy to the world! The Lord is come;

Let earth receive her King;
Let ev'ry heart prepare Him room,
And heav'n and nature sing."

(*All during the Christmas story the other choral
groups have been watching and listening in rapt
attention. Now the silence is broken.*)

CHORUS TEMPORAL.
Indeed we had lost sight of
The origin of Yule
The reason for the merriment
Forgive—we played the fool.

CHILDREN OF TOMORROW.
But wait, what of the promise
Of a glory that goes on?
You said that this *was* Christmas.
Was. Then it is gone?

CHORUS CELESTIAL—ALTOGETHER AGAIN.
It was and is and will be
Until the end of time.
Rekindled each tomorrow
Simplistic, yet sublime.
And now from all our company
With one far-reaching voice
We wish a holy Christmas
Rejoice! Rejoice! Rejoice!

(*With this conclusion of the presentation, it might
be prearranged that the entire company sing—and*

this time sing—*a final carol.* O Come All Ye Faithful *would be particularly appropriate. The curtain might remain open until the hymn is completed.*)

PRODUCTION NOTES

Choral reading offers an interesting, and often welcome, deviation from the usual group singing at Christmas time. Yet, like singing, it allows for a large number of participants. Here, because it is combined with the tableaux, it accommodates an even greater cast for a holiday program.

What Will You Tell Us of Christmas? is not, however, simply choral reading. It is reminiscent in a way of the chorus in ancient Greek drama. The Temporal and Celestial groups and the Children of Tomorrow arc characters in conflict. The story is told through them.

A word or two should be said about the manner in which the script is presented. Voice tone, volume, and intensity are mentioned sparingly. A choral director will have ideas for following through. You are not bound to the instructions given in the script. In the recounting of the nativity story, for example, a different group may take each segment of the narration, or there could be several solo speeches. Again the director can alter the presentation as he or she sees fit.

Staging can also be adjusted. Changing the set from street scene to living room to stable might be a problem since you have little time. Of course, the problem is nonexistent if you have a sophisticated theater with a revolving stage, but alternatives must be considered. As the script suggests, you could have a backdrop—a painted view of apartment doors and windows with their appropriate decorations. Behind it a part of the living room scene could be already in place. Again with the stable scene you could have a backdrop which would fall in front of the Christmas tree and the fireplace. You need only a few minutes to get father's chair and the toys and packages off into the wings.

As the script stands, the scenes on the stage are silent and motionless, but you could change that by introducing pantomime. The shoppers might offer comic situations. A child might run off to join the carolers and a mother drop her bundles as she runs to bring him back. You could add other humorous action. There could be interplay among the carolers, and you might even bring in a weary Santa with his jingling bell.

In the living room scene there is "squabbling over toys." You might do something with that. Also father is asleep. How about a loud snore? And that brings you to another consideration. If you wish, you can add dialogue. Improvisation is the thing these days. Here is an opportunity to put it into practice.

The Christmas story could be expanded. You could adhere more closely to the biblical narration which is longer (second chapter of Matthew). You might have Mary and Joseph come from the back of the theater or at least move up from one side onto the stage when they come to Bethlehem. You could do the same with the shepherds. Adding more action might liven up the program, and if necessary, you could augment the choral reading by having soft background music as the characters advance.

Since so many alternatives have been offered for expansion, it is foolish to take time to list all the props you might need or to give details of costuming. They will vary according to your adaptation. It is a tradition of the season that those in charge will scrounge around and stitch and paint and innovate for the success of the presentation.

What Will You Tell Us of Christmas? is more production than play, and there is a part for everyone who wants to be in the show. It is a project which will take time and patience and talent, but it should certainly fill the need of your school or community for a satisfying Christmas program.